Baba & Me

by

Kim Morrall

Z lyubov'yu – To my Babas – Sophie, Rose, Katherine, Donia, Anne, Mary and Flora

Special thanks to my husband John and my mom Rita for their feedback and editing, Taras for his Ukrainian expertise and Cara – or C.D. Breadner as she's known in the publishing world – for her publishing knowledge.

Table of Contents

August - A Trip to Baba's

I kept glancing over at the trees as I drove my Volkswagen down Highway 52 toward Ituna, Saskatchewan, the mid-sized town I lived in until I was thirteen and the place where my baba, Sophia Smysnuik, still lived. A slightly dour feeling came over me as I could see some of the trees were already showing the telltale signs of autumn. Summer was my favourite time of year. The warmth of the air, trips to the lake, a nice cold beer while eating barbeque outside and, being a teacher, not having to work. Life infinitely had less stress. It's not that I had an aversion to the season of autumn. The beckoning beauty of the ever changing leaves and magical, misty mornings did not go unappreciated. However, the change of seasons meant only one thing---that the long, harsh and bitterly cold Saskatchewan winter was just around the corner.

This feeling added to a sense of uneasiness I was already experiencing. The anticipation of the big announcement I was about to make made my stomach churn to the point where I felt a bit queasy. I rubbed my stomach and was struck by the thought that it was like I was rubbing Aladdin's magical lamp. I was amused at this idea, so I kept rubbing and made a wish for the best.

It's not that I thought that my baba wouldn't be happy for me. It was more my worry that my baba was not the biggest fan of my husband Josh, because he was not, in her words, "ukrayins'ke" and, therefore, perhaps not worthy of me. She never said those exact words, but I got the distinct impression that was how she felt. She would regularly announce that my children would not be truly "ukrayins'kyy" like it was some big tragedy equal to the starving kids in Africa. The fact that Josh wasn't Catholic, even though he did go to church with me, did not help matters. However, I loved my baba and it was time to tell her my big news.

My baba and I were very close when I was growing up in Ituna. I would visit her every day after school to tell her about my day. The fact that there were always freshly baked jam-jam cookies (my favourite) waiting for me may have been had something to do with it as well.

My baba was so fascinating to me at that time. She was born Sophia Rodych and she had come by herself from Ukraine when she was only seventeen years old. My gido, who was almost ten years older than her, had come three years earlier to start their life in this new country as farmers. Once he had settled and got himself established, he sent money for my Baba to come to Canada.

They had twelve children, although two of them died at a very young age, one right after the other. I asked Baba about it once and she became very serious and sullen and said it was because Mrs. Spilchuk had given her the "prystrit", the "evil eye". Apparently, they had an argument, something about gyspies being out of favour with God of all things, and Baba called Mrs. Spilchuk a "durna svynya" (a stupid pig) in front of all the church ladies.

Mrs. Spilchuk, not unexpectedly, was furious and told baba, "shliak trafiv", which I didn't learn until much later, is not a very nice thing to say to anyone either.

It was shortly after that my baba had to endure the loss of her two infant children. She had once said that she had not realized at first that Mrs. Spilchuk cursed her and her family at the time, but when she finally figured it out, she made sure Mrs. Spilchuk had stopped for good. I never knew what she meant by that, but, years later, I had heard that Mrs. Spilchuk, who was still fairly young and in seemingly good health, died in the middle of mass at St. George's Ukrainian Catholic Church of a massive heart attack.

I remember asking my mother why Baba would be so upset with Mrs. Spilchuk and she told me that she thought Baba might have had some gypsy blood in her, but because so many people discriminated against the gypsies, she would never admit to it readily. I had always thought it would be cool to have gypsy ancestry and it made my Baba even more interesting to me.

Additionally, it would have explained a lot about her. She, along with many others who came from the old country, had many superstitions and, what some may say, unconventional beliefs. I would constantly prod her for new folkloric myths during my many after school visits. I was already making sure that I didn't whistle in the house, something that, unfortunately, Josh made the mistake of doing once. Apparently this was another reason I should not have married him, or so I was told.

 I also made sure that I did not let black cats cross in front of me, walk under ladders, step on anyone's toes, hand someone a glass directly or sit on cold cement or steel. I drove my parents absolutely CRAZY by telling them all the things they should not be doing. I would say "You shouldn't leave empty plates on the table because that's bad luck" or "Dad did you carry mom over the threshold when you got married so you could prevent her from doing evil magic?" or "You guys CAN'T give the Purchas knives for a wedding present. It's bad luck!" Needless to say, they were not impressed. I sometimes wonder if they didn't move to Yorkton to get me away from Baba and her irrational superstitions.

To top it off, my baba is what is known as a Babka-Sheptukha - a folk healer, or you could say, a granny whisperer. She had started to do this while living on the farm to earn a bit of extra cash, but when my gido had passed away twenty years ago, she moved into town and took it up as a full-time job of sorts. People came from all over to see her for her special abilities.

I used to pretend she was a sorceress conjuring up magic potions in her tower to heal the sick. In essence, though, that is exactly what she was doing. She performed rituals such as "the pouring forth of wax" to treat various ailments--- most often resulting from a fearful or traumatic experience.

On a few select occasions, she allowed me to watch "the wax ritual". It always took place in her kitchen. She would ask the person to explain their health problem. Then she stood behind them while they were sitting on a chair. She held a bowl of holy water over their head while saying a prayer. She would then make the sign of the cross on the bowl with a knife and would pour melted wax into the bowl. The wax would harden and she would loosen the wax from the bowl and turn it over to interpret the shapes of the wax.

She always performed this act three times and when she was done, it was supposed to have alleviated the person's mental anxiety and fears and, of course, the health issue that emerged as a result of their traumatic experience. Unbelievably, even in this day and age, people still came to see my baba to cure their "fear sickness".

When I was younger, I loved being around my baba when she was 'working'. She just seemed so much more interesting than anybody else in the world. However, my world was pretty small at that time, but it soon became much bigger.

I was thirteen when my dad decided to give up the farm which he and my mom inherited from my gido, and move to the "big" city of Yorkton to work at, of all places, the Post Office. In hindsight, maybe it wasn't so surprising, because he had worked part time as a mail carrier when he was younger while trying to earn his Agriculture degree. Still, he was truly a man of the earth and loved farming, so to say that I was shocked by my parent's decision was a vast understatement.

Like most teenage girls, I did what I knew best. I sulked. Then I screamed and told them how much I hated them. Then I cried a million times over from the overwhelming fear of being moved from the only world I had ever known. I settled on not speaking to my parents for three whole weeks! I even ran away to my baba's and stayed there for two days determined to change their minds.

When they finally came to get me, I begged and pleaded for them to let me stay and live with my baba, but to no avail. Thus, the summer before I started high school, I reluctantly left my little world, and my baba, behind.

Little did I know how much I would change. I wasn't just leaving life in Ituna behind, I was leaving my childhood. I was growing up. Some of it would have inevitably happened anyway as I lost interest in the adults around me and became interested in boys, friends, clothes, makeup and all those things girls become interested in when they start to become adults. My world grew and I grew with it.

As I became older and attended the University of Saskatchewan, my Dad's alma mater, my world grew yet further still, until I became the complete opposite from who I was when I was thirteen. The things I had found so fascinating as a child now felt foolish as an adult. I have wondered numerous times how I would have turned out if I had stayed in Ituna. I only had to look as far as my friends that I grew up with in Ituna and who continued to live there. They all got married and had babies when they were quite young, most forgoing school and a career. I had found this peculiar, because we were forever making plans about how we couldn't wait to move out of Ituna, which we thought was "so boring", and move together to the biggest city in Saskatchewan - Saskatoon - where there was, "like, a million restaurants and movie theatres with TEN screens!" It all seems laughable now, especially given my dramatic reaction when I did have to move. I still wonder why they chose to stay and, admittedly, it often feels like we are from two different worlds now.

Whenever I mention any of them and the lives they live, my mother will try to bring me down a notch by saying, "Oy oy oy! Big city girl so much more big and important than us silly town folks!"

Why she includes herself in that statement I don't know. However, she had the last laugh when Josh and I moved from Saskatoon, a city of over 200,000, three years ago to Yorkton, a city of 15,000, so he could be a partner in his father's law firm.

I have to admit it was quite an adjustment since I had been gone almost ten years, but it was what Josh wanted to do and I, as a teacher, could work pretty much anywhere. As well, it meant I could visit my baba more often, since Ituna was only a little less than an hour away.

When all was said and done, I may have thought my baba's superstitions and folk healing were silly now, but she was my baba and she was getting older, or so she had been telling me every time I've seen her for the last twenty years. It was important to visit her as much as I could. That was my last thought as I pulled in front of her house, stopped the car and looked at the modest white house I knew so well. I took a deep breath and opened my car door.

Don't Wear Necklaces

I walked up the gravel driveway to the back of the house as Baba preferred people to go through the back. I opened the door, stepped inside and walked up the three creaky steps to the door that led into the kitchen. The door was shut and so I turned the handle to open it, but it was locked. I jiggled the rusty door handle around a bit, because it got stuck sometimes, but it still wouldn't open.

"Strange!" I thought, "She knows I'm coming."

I called out, "Baba!"

No answer.

"BABAAAA!!!"

Still no answer!

"BAAABAAAAAA!!!!"

I heard some shuffling and a low murmuring of voices, but still no one opened the door. Slightly bothered, I shouted out "SOPHIA!" Knowing it annoyed her to no end when I called her by her first name and figuring that would definitely get her to open the door. Sure enough, a few seconds later the door swiftly swung open and Baba looked down at me with a scowl on her face.

"Tykho! I'm workeeng!"

And with that she shut the door as swiftly as she opened it.

Oops! I should have known better. She always locked the kitchen door when she was with a "patient". However, I would have thought that she wouldn't be seeing anyone because she knew I was coming over.

I went back outside and into her massive garden to help myself to some peas and then sat down on a half broken, wooden lawn chair that was sitting in the middle of her lawn. Ten minutes later the back door opened and old Mr. Krywulak wobbled out.

I smiled at him and said, "Dobryy den Pan Krywulak."

"Oh hawlo, hawlo!" he muttered embarrassedly.

I always thought it was funny that when I spoke to older Ukrainian people using the little Ukrainian that I knew, they would appreciate someone speaking to them in their own language, but, without fail, they always answered back in English. I was about to inquire about his health, but he was already scooting down the driveway. For a ninety year old man, he moved incredibly fast.

I walked up the cracked, worn cement steps into Baba's house and, once again, up the steps to the kitchen and knocked on the door. I would have just walked in, but I was not about to take any chances. You never know who or what else she might have going on in there!

Baba opened the door and smiled at me as if she had not just seen me ten minutes before.

"DONIA!" she said cheerily.

"Hi Baba!" I replied.

Donia is actually my middle name. My first name is Emma, but Baba refused to call me by Emma, because, "Dat's no ukrayins'ka name! Wot is dat? Ahma? Ahma?" I personally think that because she couldn't pronounce my name correctly, she just wasn't going to bother. She couldn't pronounce Josh's name either. She called him "Yosh" a few times and then, regrettably, he made the mistake of trying to correct her. Since then, she now just says, "You there!" to him.

I leaned over to give my Baba a hug, but she backed away, pointed to the doorway and said, "No, no, no, no!"

Ah yes, how could forget? Superstition #106 - Never greet someone while standing in a door way. You must always wait until they are inside the house.

I stepped through the doorway and then hugged Baba. She felt soft and warm as my arms wrapped around and held on tightly to her fleshy body.

"Yak sya mayesh?" I hoped asking her how she was in Ukrainian would please her and I'd, at least, get a Ukrainian response from her.

"OY! I'm getting so old!"

I really don't know why I bother. This is the same answer she has given me for the last twenty years.

"My arteritees ees making my knees hurt. My blood pressure ees up again. I don't know why God doesn't just take me already?" she complained.

"Have you been taking the medications your doctor prescribed?" I inquired.

"Ach! Wot does ee know? Ee's not Ukrahnian! I have my own medicines!"

Okay then! Sometimes it was better not to argue with her, but I made a mental note to mention it to my mom later.

"So what did Mr. Krywulak want?" I asked, but already knowing the answer.

"Oh Meesus Krywulak is bugging him again!" she followed this by mumbling something in Ukrainian I couldn't quite understand, but knew by her tone it probably wasn't very nice.

The funny thing was that Mrs. Krywulak had now been dead for ten years and ever since then Mr. Krywulak has been claiming she comes and haunts him every night in his sleep.

"You'd think he would have been able to get rid of her by now," I smirked.

"Hmph!" was her only reply.

I wouldn't let up though.

"I mean how many times has he visited you now? You know what I think?" I asked.

"Wot?" she replied, pretending she wasn't in the least bit interested in my answer.

"I think Mr. Krywulak has a crush on you and he's making the whole thing up just to see you! That's what I think!" I announced triumphantly knowing it would get a rise out of her, especially since I was pretty sure she had a thing for him as well.

"Te dah! Such theengs you say!"

I giggled and gave my Baba another hug. She knew I loved to tease her and I think she secretly loved being teased.

"Deed you have lonch?" she asked.

"Yes Baba! I'm okay. Really!" I answered not knowing why I even bothered to object.

Sure enough she started to move towards the fridge, "I'll just make a leetle sometheeng!"

"Baba no! Really come sit down! I have something to tell you!" I pleaded, but she already had the stove on and was pulling out some bread.

I had no choice but to sit down. I looked around the ancient kitchen I knew so well. Nothing had really changed in Baba's kitchen in twenty years. There was still the little icon of the Virgin Mary below the crucifix of Jesus on the wall by the door. The ancient olive green fridge, always full of food, was somehow still running. The little basket of Ukrainian Easter eggs in the middle of the table and the candy bowl that sat beside it was always full of either scotch mints or hard toffees. Unless it was Christmas, when the candy bowl was full of those colourful hard candies that had little pictures of flowers or fruit in the centres of them.

I took it all in when it finally dawned on me to ask, "Do you need some help?"

"No! No! Siday! Seet!" which was followed by, "Oh Bozhe! Son of a beech!"

My baba swears quite often. Not something you'd expect to hear out of the mouth of a very religious, eighty year old woman.

"What?" I stood alarmed.

"I forget your birthday present!!" she exclaimed.

I laughed, "Oh Baba, don't worry about that!"

However, she was already rushing to her bedroom.

She came back to the kitchen and handed me a square, blue velvet jewelry box.

"Dyakuyu!" I said and opened the box.

It was a gold cross. Not unlike many of the previous ones she had given me before.

"Thank you Baba! I love it!" I said again as I was opening the clasp and putting the delicate chain around my neck, knowing full well she would think I didn't like the necklace if I didn't.

"Eet was blessed by Fr. Morris and eet's 18 carat gold," she said proudly.

Whenever my baba gave me jewelry, I was ALWAYS told it was "18 carat gold". I could never figure out why, exactly, she felt the need to mention this fact to me. Baba was not an ostentatious woman, so it baffled me why she took pride in mentioning the value of these gifts.

I asked my mom about this and she explained that Baba grew up quite poor and so giving a gift of worth was a source of pride. The fact that you could afford such things meant you were doing well and providing for your family.

"Well it's lovely," I smiled at her.

Satisfied, she went back to making lunch. I looked around the kitchen some more and wondered to myself how many times I had sat in the same spot while Baba had cooked for me. A wave of nostalgia fell over me and left me feeling a bit melancholic.

"Are you sure you don't want any help?" I asked again.

I was feeling antsy about telling Baba my news and needed something to distract me.

"NO! You seet!" she ordered. Then added, "You look tired."

It was right then I knew I had to tell her before I chickened out.

"Well there's a reason for that," I started.

Baba whipped around looking alarmed and spoke animatedly, "Oh Bozhe! Are you seek? You know I always tell you to lose weight or you going to be seek!"

She kept rambling on until, finally, I had to cut her off.

"BABA! RELAX! I'm not sick!" Then I took a deep breath and added, "I'm...pregnant."

She stared at me for what seemed like an eternity, but was probably only a few seconds.

Then she spoke, "Oh Donia!"

I could see tears filling her eyes. She put her big, well worn hands on my arms, grabbed tightly and smiled the biggest smile imaginable. Then she wrapped her arms around my body to give me the biggest hug she had ever given me.

When she let go, she grabbed my arms again and said, "You must make sure not to wear necklace."

WHAT???

"Come! Come!"

She was now reaching over the table to get the jewelry box that had held the cross.

"Take eet off!" she ordered.

"Baba! Why?" I asked completely confused.

"Ees bad luck!" she explained.

"Oh! Okay then!"

I knew better than to argue, so I took it off and handed it to Baba.

Then she made her way to her "special" cupboard and pulled out a bottle of her "finest" horilka.

"Baba I can't!" I told her.

"Why not?" she asked obliviously.

"I'm pregnant! Remember?"

"Te deh!" She said waving her hand at me.

Drinking vodka to celebrate good news is a really strong Ukrainian tradition and to refuse a drink, especially when one was being congratulated or blessed, was not only considered rude, but bad luck. Therefore, I didn't have much choice.

She pulled out two shot glasses, which were actually the little medicinal measuring cups you get when you buy cough syrup, and poured the horilka. Before taking the smallest sip I could of the pungent, very strong homemade brew, Baba offered me congratulations and blessings.

We raised our glasses and she said, "Dli Doni, bazhaiu shchob Boh zberih vas i vashoii dytyny vid zla." Or "To Donia, I wish that God protects you and your baby from harm."

"Day Bozhe!" I replied.

"Day Bozhe!" she replied back.

It felt like a weight had been lifted from me now that Baba knew and I could breathe a lot easier. I actually felt pretty foolish for being so worried about the whole thing in the first place.

Baba realized her soup was boiling over and so as soon as the toast was done, she put her "glass" down and went right back to making lunch.

"That woman never misses a beat!" I thought to myself.

The rest of the afternoon was spent in enjoyable, and somewhat entertaining, conversation. Baba asked me a thousand questions about how I was feeling. She found it hard to believe I didn't have any morning sickness. She also regaled me with stories about when she was pregnant. Some I found to be somewhat doubtful, like when she gave birth to my Uncle Orest while milking the cows.

"Baba! That did not happen!" I countered.

"Tak! Yes! I seemply wipe your oncle and give him to your Auntie Olga to take eenside the house."

"And what did you do then?" I asked incredulously.

"I went back to meelking the cows of course!" she answered, "Wot else you theenk I'd do??"

"BABA!" I shook my head at her, "There is NO way that happened!"

"Tak! Tak! Wot you theenk?" she said, "I had work to do!"

I laughed and laughed at the crazy stories she told me and it felt good.

When it came to say good-bye, I kissed her on her bright pink cheek and hugged her tightly feeling the warmth of her soft body against mine. Before I left I promised to keep in touch and that I would visit again soon.

I made a quick stop to my good friend Deanna's house before I left Ituna to drop off a book she had wanted to read. I told her my news.

"Congratulations sweetie!" she squawked trying to make herself heard over her two scrapping boys and wiping off her youngest daughter's sticky, paint-filled hands.

"Now you'll understand," she quipped sounding like some Middle Eastern sage.

Her eyes appeared to be both smiling and laughing at the same time.

I knew what she meant and it kept me preoccupied as I was driving home. All my girlfriends from Ituna have been mothers for years. I had always felt a little left out when they spoke about being pregnant and all of their baby experiences.

"Not anymore!" I thought as I rubbed my belly full of life...and Baba's delicious borscht.

I smiled and took a deep breath, and as I was driving by the same trees I had passed earlier, I foolishly reflected to myself, "Now I can relax!"

Don't Touch Your Face When You've Been Frightened

The next day I woke up still feeling relaxed and upbeat. I chided myself for how much unnecessary stress I had put myself through. Much to my dismay, I was a perpetual worrier. I consistently vowed to be one of those zen-like, carefree individuals who let the troubles of the world bounce off them without a thought. Unfortunately, I was just not built that way.

After Josh left for work, I decided to take a bath. It was a particularly cool day and it had left me feeling chilled. I slipped into the tub and allowed myself to be hugged by the warm, inviting water. As I laid in in the tub, I thought about the changes my body was going through with mixed feelings. I wasn't really showing yet, but I felt different somehow. I felt more alive and, well, special. The idea that I had this little being inside me was so wondrous, but yet so scary at the same time.

Women never tell you about that---being scared I mean. Whenever you see these movies or commercials about couples finding out they are pregnant, they are always so jubilant. When we first found out, my reaction was much more subdued and pensive. It wasn't that I didn't feel happiness, but, at the same time, I also felt slightly apprehensive. It was quite surprising to me that I would feel this way.

I swished the lovely, warm water over my belly and wondered what it was going to feel like in a few months when the baby started getting bigger. The idea of having this little person kicking me from the inside was unimaginable. As I was dwelling in my thoughts, the phone started to ring.

"Shit!" I muttered aloud.

I had forgotten to take the portable phone with me into the bathroom. I contemplated whether or not I should get out of the tub. I'm one of those people who hates not answering the phone. Josh always lets the phone ring if he doesn't feel like answering, or if he is just being too lazy to pick it up. It drives me crazy! I decided that the thought of getting out into the cold air was worse than missing the call. I hoped the person would leave a message. The phone clicked onto the answering machine and I strained to listen and hear the message through the closed door.

"HAWLO!"

Baba!

"Oh son of a beech! I hate these theengs!"

I smiled and chuckled to myself.

"Donia! I forget to tell you, don't ever touch your face when you get frightened. Okay? Or else your baby weel have birthmark on the face."

What the hell?

"Okay I go! Meester Krywulak ees coming over! Meesus Krywulak gave him good scare last night!"

With that she hung up. I chuckled again and shook my head while thinking, "Okay that was weird!" I know I grew up with my baba and her crazy superstitions as a child, but I had not had a real taste of them since I was 13. It was amusing, but a bit disconcerting at the same time.

The water had cooled, so I pulled the plug and stepped out. I immediately went to the phone and called my mom.

"Hey!" I said before she could even say hello back. "What the hell is this thing about not touching your face when you get scared or else your baby will get a birthmark?"

"What?" she asked confused.

"Touching your face! When pregnant! You're not supposed to touch your face when you get frightened or else you'll get a birthmark?"

"Oh yeah!" she laughed, "I forgot you went to see mom yesterday."

"No, she called me just now to relay that precious jewel of wisdom on me. Funny that I haven't ever read that in any of my pregnancy books," I remarked sarcastically.

My mom laughed again and just said, "Well then aren't you lucky to have someone like your baba to keep you informed."

"Oh yes! Very lucky!!" I muttered.

"How is mom?" she asked.

It's still odd to me to think of Baba as being my mother's mom. I can't in any way, shape or form picture my mother as a child.

"Fine," I said, "But she's not taking her medications, at least I don't think she's taking them."

"Oh Bozhe!" was her response.

"You sounded EXACTLY like Baba right now," I giggled.

My dad is constantly telling my mom how much she is becoming like my baba. I'm not entirely sure she is pleased about that.

"Anyways," she said changing the subject, "I'll be able to check on her on Wednesday. I'm going to Ituna to help her make perogies and cabbage rolls for Thanksgiving. Wanna come?" she asked.

"Can't! Gotta doctor's appointment," I responded, thankful that I had a reason not to go.

I hated making perogies and cabbage rolls. Nothing bored me to tears more. Eating them, however, was a different story.

"Okay then, I guess that you just saw her anyway," she answered, putting on her best disappointed voice that she always used when she was trying to guilt me into doing something she wanted.

"Yep!" I replied curtly, "Sorry, I have to go!" Thinking that I had better get off the phone before she had me making another trip to Ituna. "I have a lunch date with the girls."

"Okay then. Have a good time," she replied still using her disappointed voice.

"Thanks! Bye Mom!"

I hung up before she could say another word.

Close one! I love both my mom and my baba, but together I could only handle them in small doses. Between the worrying and nagging and the constant "advice", it was enough to drive even the Dalai Lama bonkers.

I dried off and started to get ready for my lunch. I have a group of four girlfriends from my high school days in Yorkton that I am still friends with and we tried to make sure we went out every couple of weeks for lunch or coffee to catch up on each other's lives. I cherished this time as it gave me a chance to bitch about whatever was stressing me out - husband, job, family, etc., and I knew I would be supported wholeheartedly. I knew I'd especially be supported now as all my friends had babies and had gone through all the madness.

I met the girls at noon at a place we frequented quite often called Sweet Treats, an amazing little dessert place that also served fantastic lunches.

As we were looking at the menu trying to figure out what to order I told them, "So I officially broke the news to my baba yesterday."

"Oh oh!" Angie, my closest friend in the group, was the first to respond.

Angie understood me better than anyone else. It was like we were on the same wavelength. We became close in high school when I found out that we both had a deep love of Barbara Streisand. We'd often sit for hours on this big hill in front of her house talking about life while consuming vast amounts of peanut M&Ms and Big Gulps filled with Diet Coke.

We called it our "hill nights". I miss those moments sometimes. Not that you could get her to do that now. Angie was a fitness instructor who loved working out and playing sports and she rarely ate anything that wasn't good for her.

"How'd she take it?" asked Melissa.

Melissa was one of my first friends in Yorkton and the most pragmatic of the bunch. She was a computer tech for the Yorkton Health District. Melissa was one of those people who wanted to be a mom in high school, so it wasn't surprising that she married young and got pregnant almost immediately thereafter.

"Good!" I answered, "Surprisingly good!"

"Well that's good, cuz we don't want a bitchy Baba!" Linda joked.

Linda was the friend who made me laugh the most. She could turn any story into a comedy routine. I had always thought she'd become a professional singer because she had the most beautiful voice, but she surprised us all by becoming a nurse.

"She has given me some weird advice though, " I said while still laughing at Linda's remark.

"Of course she did!" Angie responded.

"No, I mean she told me not to wear necklaces as soon as she found out."

"I see you took her advice to heart," Melissa remarked sarcastically as she looked at the big, sparkly necklace I was wearing.

What could I say? I LOVE my jewelry! I was always wearing bold statement necklaces or sparkly cocktail rings or big, flashy earrings. They were a part of my identity in a way.

"Whatever!" I retorted in mock annoyance and continued, "She also called this morning to tell me not to touch my face when I got frightened."

They all looked at me confused for a moment and finally Sandy asked, "WHY?"

I had met Sandy a little later than the rest of my friends, but we became fast friends once we got to know each other. She shared my penchant for shoes, many of which I inherited after she'd given birth because they didn't fit her anymore. I was already praying that the same thing didn't happen to me. God! What would I do with all my shoes??? Sandy was peculiar in that even after drinking and partying all night, she would make you get up early to go to church with her, so I wasn't surprised that the superstition thing caught her interest first. Sandy had some pretty strong views about religion and God.

"Because the baby will get a birthmark on the place I touch."

Silence.

"What the hell?" Angie finally responded.

"I'm not sure exactly, but it's my Baba and you know her with her superstitions and folk healing rituals and all that."

"She shouldn't do those things," Sandy chirped in.

Here we go!

"I'm surprised she does that stuff, being so religious."

"It is what it is," I replied tersely, "besides when she performs the rituals, she is always praying and asking for God's hand in helping...or...whatever!"

I felt the need to defend my baba even though technically I had just been complaining about her.

"My advice is to just let her tell you these things and then do what you want," Melissa advised.

"Yeah! Just don't wear any of your big, honkin necklaces in front of her and you'll be fine!" Linda chuckled.

"NOOOOOO!!! NO, NO, NO!" Angie barked. "If you start letting people boss you around, you'll never hear the end of it! Next thing you know you'll be bombarded with all sorts of unwanted advice. They'll be telling you what NOT to eat, what NOT to wear, what you should NOT say and NOT do and it will drive you CRAZY!"

Angie came from a large Ukrainian family as well, so she understood, more than the rest, what I was going through.

"But this is her BABA were talking about," Linda reminded her.

True! It's not like I could tell my baba to bugger off or anything of the sort.

"Don't tell them what you're naming the baby!" Sandy, all of a sudden, piped in.

"Oh God yeah!"

"Definitely!"

"YES!"

"Okay, why?" I asked.

"Just trust us!" Melissa, in her wisest voice, informed me.

"And for God's sake, don't let them convince you to cut your hair. It's not that bad having long hair with babies," Linda added in for good measure.

"Well I'm not quite there yet," I laughed, "but you don't ever have to worry about that!"

One of the other things that defined me was my long, wavy hair. I have never had short hair and I was not about to start now as it, sadly, was the only thing I ever got compliments for when it came to my body.

The rest of the lunch continued to be "advice" on what "advice" not to take. I felt better and I had decided to take Melissa's suggestion about letting Baba continue, but I would just basically ignore what she said. Easy enough! Right??? Honestly, I wasn't so sure.

Two days later, I went for my doctor's appointment. I decided to mention my baba's warning 'just in case'. Just in case of what I'm not sure, but I thought it couldn't hurt.

He stared at me blankly for a second and then retorted, "That's ridiculous!"

Don't hold back now! Geez!

"Okay," I answered back feeling more than a bit foolish.

He changed the subject quickly since he obviously felt he couldn't be bothered with my silliness any more.

"Are you going back to teach?" he asked.

"Yes. I start tomorrow," I replied, "I don't know why they don't just wait until after the long weekend," I added, trying to make small talk.

"Hmm!" was his only response.

He was busy typing information into his computer. I don't know why he ever bothered asking me anything. He never seemed the least bit interested in any of my answers.

He helped me up since I had been lying on my back the whole time.

Then, with an austere look, he said, "Your body is going through major changes right now. That's not always easy to deal with. You're also going to have situations that are going to be stressful. You'll just have to remember to think of your health and, of course, the baby's health and you'll be fine."

"Yes of course. Sounds good," I answered.

Oh yes. So easy. Such simple advice. Think of my and the baby's health and everything else will be swell. Gee why didn't think of that? I forced a smile in response, thanked him and went on my merry way.

Later on, while I was making supper, Josh came home. He kissed me on the cheek while I was stirring the spaghetti sauce.

"Hmmmm, yummy!"

Spaghetti was his favourite meal.

"How was your day?" I asked.

"Hmmm," he responded.

I sighed but tried again, "Anything exciting happen?"

"Nope," as was his usual response.

I sighed again. Sometimes trying to get Josh to talk was exasperating!

Finally, he asked, "How did your appointment go?"

"Good! Everything looks good!" I answered.

"And how did Dr. Rens look?" he teased.

"Shut up!" I grumbled at him embarrassed.

I have to admit I have a "slight" crush on my doctor. The man might not have much of a personality, but he is terribly good looking. I made the mistake of mentioning this once to Josh and he has bugged me about him ever since.

"Oh admit it, you love getting examined by your tall, dark, handsome doctor!" he tormented me some more.

"You know what? I'm in close proximity to many, many very sharp knives and I have some pretty wacky hormones right now, so I'd watch out if I were you!" I threatened.

"Are you going to use the hormone excuse for everything now?" he grumbled.

"Shush!" I barked. "Go take your suit off! Supper is almost ready."

Josh went upstairs whistling to annoy me some more. I finished making supper, but, I have to admit, with a big smile on my face.

Ahh, Dr. Rens!!

Don't Do Any Spinning

The next morning was my first day back at work.
The students weren't back yet, thank goodness, but
it was still beyond depressing to have to return,
especially when it was still so beautiful outside.

The morning was pure chaos and confusion. Josh
was already at work and I was scrambling around
trying to put on my makeup and find my keys at
the same time. I'm not at all a morning person and
having been able to sleep in all summer didn't help
matters. Between this and the fact that I had
trouble sleeping last night meant that I slept in.
Josh came into our room just before he left for
work to give me a kiss.

"Don't you have work this morning?" he asked.

I bolted up, threw on my glasses, and looked at the
time.

"WHY didn't you wake me up?" I yelled.

"Sorry!" he said sheepishly, "I knew you had
trouble sleeping, so I thought I'd let you get some
extra rest."

"Are you serious? On my first day back to work?"
I barked.

Josh just stared and said nothing which is what he usually does when I'm yelling at him. Another thing that drives me CRAZY!!! My family is always yelling at each other, so I'm used to it. Josh, however, comes from a family that never raised their voices, so whenever I yell at him, he completely shuts down. I told him once that I thought his parents should have done him a favour and hollered at him every once in a while, which may seem like an odd thing to say to someone, but I was completely serious. The guy cannot handle anger of any kind, so he just tends to ignore or internalize everything. I'm not saying it is healthy to be screaming either, but at least you are releasing your anger. At least that's what I like to tell myself!

I would have liked to continue my tirade, but I had to get ready, so I just shook my head at him and told him to go away. He knew better than to stay.

Now here I was five minutes before the first staff meeting of the year and I'm running around with a tube of lipstick in one hand and rummaging around my purse looking for my bloody keys with the other.

"Shit! Shit! Shit!"

I had a brief thought that the baby could hear me and I shouldn't really be swearing, so I apologized to my belly, "Sorry baby!"

I have to admit I can be pretty vulgar at times. I have tried in the past to curb the cursing, but to no avail. This wasn't the best time to start forming better habits either.

My mother loves to scold me when I swear. I realize it is not an endearing quality in a person, but her nagging me about it always makes me want to swear even more. I fully realize this makes me sound like a petty thirteen year old girl. However, when she says things like "You know I never swear!" or "You sound like a truck driver". It just brings out the worst in me. Besides it felt good to let out all my frustrations this way. The added plus of annoying my mother was just the cherry on the top.

"Agh! Dammit!"

I stood still for a second and tried to remember what I had done with my keys.

"Think!"

Sure enough it came to me. I had put them on the counter of the bathroom when I had come home from my doctor's appointment yesterday. I had to pee really badly and ran straight into the house and into the bathroom without putting my keys down until I got into the bathroom.

I grabbed my keys and looked in the mirror.

"Well it will have to do," I mumbled to myself.

I grabbed a banana and a granola bar so I wouldn't be starving during the meeting and, as I was on my way out, the phone rang.

"SHIT! Leave it!" I told myself.

I kept going to the door, but my stupid, obsessive need to answer the phone overcame me. I looked at the call display - Baba! Damn! I contemplated for a second what to do, but, before I knew it, I had pressed talk on the phone.

"Hi Baba!" I said.

There was a brief, confused pause on the other line.

"How you know eet was me?" she asked.

"Call display Baba!" I answered.

"Call what?" she asked sounding even more confused.

"Call display! It shows who is calling you on your phone," I told her.

"I've never heard of such a theeng," she replied incredulously, and added some Ukrainian word I had never heard before.

I realized that I needed to hurry her along so I said, "Baba I'm REALLY late for work. Is there something important you need to tell me or can I call you back later?"

"Oh no! Eets wery important," she said decidedly.

"Okay!" I replied.

Silence.

"What is it Baba?" I asked somewhat impatiently.

"Oh yes! Make sure you do not do any speening," she said in a very slow, deliberate manner so as to make sure I was fully aware of what she was saying.

It did not help.

"Any what?" I asked bewildered.

"Speening. SPEENING!" she repeated.

"Spinning?" I still wasn't sure.

"Yes! Speening! Like around and around!" she clarified.

"Oh spinning!" I finally understood...maybe.

"Uh, why not?" I asked.

"Ees bad!" was her only explanation. It was followed by, "Okay I go!" and she hung up.

Shit! Shit! Shit!

I walked into our staff meeting a full twenty minutes late. I foolishly thought that I might get away with it too, but Tad Keens, the music teacher at the school, made sure this was not to be.

"Hey Em! How was your summer?"

Of course he did it on purpose, and thought he was being funny. Everyone turned to look at me, including John Morales, our principal, who glared at me with his squinty, malevolent eyes which added to my embarrassment.

"Nice of you to join us Ms. Gibb."

Shit!

"Sorry! I, uh, um..." I bumbled on while Tad smiled like the jerk that he was.

All I could think was how I was going to take his stupid guitar and hit him over the head with it. I could have too, because he actually brought it to the meeting!! What was he thinking? That he'd just break into song in between discussions about staff changes and class expectations? Really I should not have been that surprised because Tad was the sort of guy who would do anything for attention. The "teaching thing" was a sideline "gig" for him until he became the famous rock star he felt he was going to be one day. He was always testing new songs on me. I hated to admit it, but they were usually quite good. Not that I would give him the satisfaction of knowing that. The man had an ego the size of Russia. He didn't need me to make himself feel good. Don't get me wrong, I liked Tad quite a bit. He was extremely funny and a pretty smart guy. He was also always good for starting interesting conversations, but his need for attention got on my nerves from time to time. It didn't help that I was feeling particularly hormonal that morning and Mr. Morales was still glaring at me waiting for an explanation.

I finally said, "My Baba called me on my way out and I couldn't get her off the phone."

It was all I could come up with and it was partly true. I sat down quickly while watching Morales shake his head at me, but, luckily, he didn't say anything else. He's been known to yell at staff members for long periods of time in front of everyone until they break down or even quit on occasion. I seriously despised him. I looked over at my friend Janie, who gave me an empathetic smile. Crazy and wonderful Janie was the Drama teacher and one of my closest friends at the school. She said EXCELLENT in a big, loud voice at lot. A LOT!!! My other friend at work was Cindy, who taught English. She made me laugh more than anyone, and I considered her a bit of a partner-in-crime, because we've gotten into trouble more than once together. She also shared in my love for Abba, which no one else seemed to understand, so she was pretty much perfect in my eyes.

She looked at me and rolled her eyes. I laughed, silently, to myself. No point in feeding the dragon!

After what seemed like hours, the meeting finished. I stood up to go to my classroom, when Morales called out to me in his best authoritative voice, "Ms. Gibb, meet me in my office in five minutes."

"Someone is in trouble!" Tad teased me.

"I hope all your guitar strings break off," I snapped back.

"Ooohhh!!!" he replied back clutching his heart in mock indignation.

"Shut up!" I hissed punching him in the arm.

He laughed and went on his merry, annoying way. I picked up my bag and walked apprehensively to Morale's office. The door was slightly ajar, so I knocked a couple of times while pushing open the door. Morales was sitting at his desk filling out some form. When I entered, he looked up at me over his glasses which were perched at the end of his nose.

"Ms. Gibb, have a seat," he ordered.

Assuming I was there so he could lecture me on the disrespectfulness of being tardy, I figured I should try to alleviate the situation as much as I could.

"How was your summer?" I asked cheerfully.

He glanced up at me dimly and without interest, and with the least amount of enthusiasm he could muster he muttered, "Fine."

"Okay, that's not going to work," I thought, "Better to try a head on approach," I decided.

"Look I'm really sorry about this morning. It was just one of those mornings where nothing was going right," I babbled.

I took a second to see if I was making any headway, but he didn't even appear to be listening as he was still writing on the form. I decided to keep rambling on.

"I slept in because Josh didn't wake me up, and then I couldn't find my keys ANYWHERE. I'm sure I spent twenty minutes looking for the damn things! And when I finally was about to leave my baba called, I just couldn't get her off the phone," I explained.

Not exactly the truth, but he didn't need to know that. He finally looked up at me and...SMILED!

"Wow!" I thought to myself, "It actually worked!"

I really should know better by now.

Morales leaned back in his chair and started to speak

"Mrs. Lekach has decided to take early retirement."

"Uh, okay."

I was totally confused now and he was obviously relishing in my confusion, because he actually smiled at me again and that man NEVER smiles. Good thing too, because it wasn't a pretty sight!

He continued on, "We've not been able to find a replacement yet, so I've had to redistribute her classes."

I could see where this was going and I felt my chest tightening, but I said nothing.

He kept going, "You'll be teaching her English Gr. 10A class."

"WHAT?" I bellowed much too loudly. I tried to recover quickly and calmly said, "But I've never taught that class before. That may not be the best idea on such short notice."

I couldn't believe it! My head started pounding. It is the curse of Fine Arts teachers to have to teach a non-Fine Arts class. Well…it was my curse anyway. I wasn't particularly fond of teaching English. There were too many papers to read and correct. In addition, with all the texting going on these days, the student's grammar has become increasingly atrocious. I really couldn't imagine anything worse. If I had to teach anything, I would have preferred Math. Math was straightforward at least. I was fortunate enough to have avoided, for the most part, teaching English and just had to teach a few low grade Math classes for the past few years. It wasn't ideal, but anything was better than trying to teach Chaucer to a bunch of disinterested fifteen year olds, especially when you weren't particularly interested in it yourself.

I decided to reiterate my dissatisfaction with the situation.

"But I've never taught Gr. 10A before, you can hardly expect me to be fully prepared in five days!" I whined.

"I'm sure you'll do fine."

His disinterest in my plight was palpable. However, I wasn't giving in so easily.

"What about my Math class then? I assume it's been reassigned?" I hoped against hope.

"Nope!" he said quite matter-of-factly.

"What about my free period?"

I was getting indignant by now, because I LIVED for my free period.

All high school teachers were mandated to have one free period in which they could use to catch up on work like correcting, assignments and lesson plans.

"Ms. Gibb, many other teachers here are in the same situation. With government cutbacks, there's nothing I can do at this point."

At this point??? At this point, I was plotting murder.

"What about substitutes?" I asked the obvious.

"That possibility was considered, but I've recently decided that it would be better for the students to have a regular teacher."

He was enjoying this way too much and I had had enough. By now, not only was my chest tight and my head pounding, but I felt a bit nauseated, which made me even more angry, so much so that I made a rash decision.

I hadn't planned on telling him about my pregnancy for at least another month or so. Josh and I felt it would be better to wait until I had fully passed my first trimester, but I was too angry to think rationally at this point. I really just wanted to make his life as equally miserable as mine was at that point.

I regained my composure and in my sweetest voice said, "Speaking of substitutes and reassigning classes, you can expect to be doing more of that this spring."

"What do you mean?" Morales asked in an irritable tone.

I suddenly felt much better as I delivered my big news to him.

"Well," I said slowly, wanting to prolong the pain, "I'm pregnant! Due in March!"

Victory! His face turned completely red and I could have sworn I saw a vein pulsating out of his neck. Principals hated nothing more than having to find a suitable teacher to take over a class so late in the school year, especially in classes that require such specific skills such as Art. I was full of glee!!!

He looked like he wanted to clobber me over the head with one of his many precious football trophies he kept in the cabinet behind him. What made it even better was that all he could say was "Congratulations" in the most unenthusiastic voice imaginable.

"Well I better go prepare," I said rising up from my chair smiling the whole time.

As soon as I left his office though, the smile vanished. I immediately went to see Cindy. I usually turned to her when I was in desperate need of teaching assistance. Even though I was pretty sure I had read most of the required curriculum when I was in high school, there was no way I remembered anything about The Grapes of Wrath or Twelfth Night or whatever was required in Gr. 10A English. Leave it to that miserable man to give me a class I had never taught before. I had taught Gr. 9A English once, so at least I could have relied on my past notes, but no, he would have to give me Gr. 10. The cretin had probably known about this all summer too!

She was organizing textbooks. I made sure I closed the door behind me, because I knew there was more than one teacher at our school who would gladly inform Morales of my impeding offensive language.

"THAT SON-OF-A-BITCH!!!!"

"I know!" she replied empathetically.

"He gave me the freaking Gr. 10A English class!" I grumbled.

"I know," she replied again.

"I have NO free period!"
I think I may have been yelling at this point.

"I know! He's a jerk! What can I tell ya?" she
squeezed my hand.

She didn't really need to say anything because I
knew she was always there for me. She was a great
ear for when I needed to vent.

"I'll need the curriculum and any notes you have,"
I requested.

"I'll bring them to you when I get through this
mess," she pointed to a mound of textbooks.

"Thanks babe!" I gave her a hug, "You're a
lifesaver!"

I started walking to the door, when a thought hit
me.

"By the way," I started, "which of Lekach's classes
did you get?"

She paused, "Gr. 9A." she sighed.

"SON-OF-A BITCH!"

"I know!"

That evening I was making macaroni and hotdogs. Not my favourite, but it was easy to make and I needed to make something quick so I could get back to preparing for my classes. I had no idea if Josh was even going to be home for supper since he had gone to a town called Canora that day for court. Several attempts at calling him proved to be unsuccessful, which added to my crusty mood.

I decided to give myself a break and call my mom to complain about my day.

"Hey it's me!" I said when she picked up.

"Hi! How's it going? How was work?" she inquired.

"TERRIBLE!" I replied.

"Why?" she sounded concerned.

"John Morales is a total dickhead!" was my not so classy answer to her question.

"Emma!"

"He hates me!" I claimed.

"He does not!" she countered.

"It's true!" I insisted.
"Why would you think that?" she asked.

I went into a lengthy diatribe about the events of my day and all she could think to say was, "Why did Baba call?"

"Oh you'll love this," I replied, "She told me I should make sure I didn't do any spinning."

"Any what?" she asked sounding just as confused as I did this morning.

"Any spinning, or speening, as she would say it."

"You mean like on one of those exercise bikes?"

You could tell she was perplexed.

"Nooo! Like going around in circles, like we did when we were kids. At least I think that's what she meant."

Now I was perplexed as well. She didn't say anything right away, then came out with, "Speaking of spinning, your sister has my head spinning."

Unbelievable! I can be in the middle of a discussion with my mom about one thing and then, without notice, she'll respond on a completely different topic. She does this when she doesn't feel like talking about what you were discussing anymore and, instead, would rather talk about something that interests her. More often than not, it was about my lovely sister and whatever shenanigans she had gotten herself into at the time. I love my sister. She's charming, lots of fun and as cute as a button, if you can even say that about a seventeen year old. However, she's got the maturity level of a four year old and an equally low level of responsibility to match. She was almost twelve years my junior and I often felt more like a second mother to her than a sister. Obviously my mother thought this as well, because she kept insisting on enlightening me to whatever current "crisis" Krissy was in and seeking advice from me on what to do with her. Not that I wasn't concerned, but I often felt my parents enabled her way too much. For instance, she once took my mom's car without permission and got into an accident. Did they ground her? No! Did they make her pay it back? No! Did they call the police? Definitely not! No, what they decided is that if she was that desperate for a car they would buy her one!!! I was flabbergasted! If that had been me, I would still not be seeing the light of day. How could you not punish such behaviour? While I did not necessarily agree with Josh's suggestion that they charge her, doing nothing and, ultimately rewarding her was even more insane.

Unfortunately, that sort of thing happened all the time with my sister. I have told my mom time and time again she needed to put her foot down and let Krissy fall on her ass, or, at the very least, she should give it a good kick! My mother had trouble letting her fail though. I think she was convinced that Krissy would forever be scarred and never be able to live a full and happy life if she did. I was of the opinion that Krissy was a conniving little brat who knew exactly what to say and do to get what she wanted.

"What now?" I said exasperated.

There was no point in pulling her back to my problems once she started on about my sister. She went on and on - something to do with Krissy's current boyfriend Greg, or Doofus as I privately called him. It was a pretty accurate description of his personality. She was chattering on and on about how he never comes into their house to say hello and how Krissy never has him come over for supper, when Josh, thankfully, walked through the front door.

"Mom!" I cut her off, "Josh is home and I need to talk to him about my day since you're so interested."

"Oh well of course I'm interested. It's just that...," she started in on the defensive, but I cut her off again before she could go too far.

"Don't worry about it and don't worry about Doo, I mean Greg," I said almost slipping up. "It's not like she'll marry him," I reasoned.

"But I just don't get why he won't visit with us," she whined.

Unbelievable!

"Okay gotta go. Talk to you later," I finished the conversation before she got going again.

"Oh okay, bye hon!" she said.

"Bye Mom!" and I hung up.

Josh looked tired from all the driving he had to do, but very cute in his old grey overcoat with half the buttons hanging off by a thread. His hair, however, cut in an awful style right out of a bad 80's movie, and which he refused to change despite constant pleading on my end, still looked perfectly coiffed as usual. I smiled. Josh had a thing about his hair. When we first started dating, I'd often have to wait an hour for him to do his hair, which was an exact replica of Barry Gibb's hairstyle, but bigger, much to my chagrin.

"Hey," he said as he bent down his tired six foot five frame for a kiss, "How was your day?"

"Terrible!" I grumbled, but not before taking my hand and rubbing it around his head.

"Hey! Don't mess the do!" he yelled, sounding like a prissy little girl.

I rolled my eyes and said, "Whatever! Let's talk about my shithead principal!"

"Okay then!" Josh replied amused at my anger.

I regaled him with day's events as he helped himself to a drink. When I was done he clearly was as unimpressed as I was.

"What a jerk!" he commented.

"I KNOW!" I exclaimed, "I still can't believe it, especially this late in the game! And then to have the nerve to tell me he is only thinking about the students??? Bullshit!"

"You'll be fine!" he reassured me as he grabbed me by the waist and put his long arms around my body.

"I'm sure I will be, but it's just that I'm so bloody tired all the time right now and it's making me incredibly bitchy!" I confessed.

"Really? I hadn't noticed," Josh joked.

"Shush you!" I warned threatening him with a spoonful of macaroni.

"I'm going to change," Josh announced starting to make his way up the stairs.

He paused for a second and asked, "So what did Baba want?"

I looked at him and smiled a little, knowing he'd find my answer amusing given the day's events.

"She told me not to do any spinning."

"Spinning?" he said with a quizzical look on his face.

"YEP! Spinning. Like this."

I gave him a demonstration.

Josh scrunched up his eyebrows like he does sometimes when he's thinking really hard, but then his eyes lit up and he smiled.

"Ah!" he simply stated and then shook his head a little as he headed upstairs where I could hear him laughing out loud.

Don't Reach for Anything Above Your Head

Josh and I were driving down the highway towards Ituna on a frosty Thanksgiving afternoon. I kept changing the station on the radio.

After a while Josh had enough, "Just pick a station already!"

"No one makes good music anymore!" I complained miserably.

Josh huffed, but didn't say anything.

I wasn't done my rant though, "IT'S LIKE NOBODY CAN BE BOTHERED TO SIT DOWN FOR A MINUTE AND COME UP WITH A DECENT SONG!!!" my whining getting louder and louder.

Josh sighed. His mouth was tensed up and you could tell he was trying his hardest not to say anything that would set me off.

He managed to calmly say, "What's wrong baby?"

"Nothing!" I grumbled.

Of course nothing could be further from the truth. As we drove to Ituna for our annual Thanksgiving supper at Baba's, I had time to think about the past month and a half. Practically every day my Baba had called me with a new piece of "advice" or word of warning about things I should or should not be doing while I was pregnant. While I certainly didn't believe in any of these old superstitions, I still found myself hesitating a little before doing things I would normally have no trouble doing.

Every time there was a new warning, I found myself getting more and more stressed out. Dr. Rens warned me that I needed to relax, but I just couldn't seem to calm down. I was worried about what would happen if things continued the way they were going.

"It will be fine," Josh said breaking my train of thought.

"What?" I asked confused.

"It will be fine," he repeated.

"No I heard that part," I said. "What will be fine?"

"You know...supper," I could tell he didn't really want to talk about it for fear of getting me started up again.

He had heard enough already.

"Yeah right!" I said harshly, "Twenty eight of my relatives in Baba's small, cramped house telling me everything they think they know about being pregnant."

"Some do," Josh offered.

I glared at him, "Oh please! Having babys a million years ago is a LOT different than having babies now!"

"Look you need to settle down. Remember what Dr. Rens told you," Josh said trying to temper, well, my temper.

"Yes I know," I took some deep breaths.

"Just remember that they are just trying to be helpful," Josh smiled at me.

"Yes, so helpful, because spinning around in circles is the first thing I want to do every morning when I wake up," I mocked, but it did put a smile on my face and I laughed.

Josh started laughing too.

"It really will be fine you know."

I, however, was not so hopeful.

"We'll see!"

When we walked into Baba's house, it was in typical form. The men were sitting in the living room drinking copious amounts of my Uncle Orest's home brew while watching a hockey game and arguing very loudly about the weather, this year's crops and whatever was pissing them off about the government these days. Listening to Ukrainians argue is like a game of one upmanship. My Gido used to say, "Two Ukrainians, three opinions!"

Of course, also in typical fashion, the women were cooking and preparing the meal in the kitchen. It was equally as loud and noisy.

As we were taking our coats off, my Uncle Orest yelled out, "Holy smokes! Look at how fat you're getting!"

I looked at Josh and we just smiled at each other. Ukrainians, at least the ones I know, typically talk about six things: along with the weather, the government and the crops. They also like to talk about the church, the family and how fat or tall you are. Oh yes, I was SO looking forward to this evening!

Josh squeezed my hand and then headed over to the couch while making his apologetic face. He knew how I felt about the whole men sitting in the living room and women working their asses off in the kitchen to serve their men thing. I glared at him and shook my head.

I hadn't even made it to the kitchen and I could see that Josh already had a drink in his hand. I could also hear my Uncle Nestor asking Josh what he thought about the raise the judges got and those lousy government taxes.

Before I stepped into the kitchen, I took a deep breath and told myself to "just relax". I walked in and said hi to everyone. My Auntie Olga immediately charged towards me and gave me a kiss.

"OY YOY YOY! How's my girl?" she asked while pinching my cheek like I was seven.

My Auntie Olga has a voice like one of those electric hand saws grinding through a piece of wood, but she was the sweetest woman in the world and only ever had positive things to say about everyone.

"Good Auntie! How are you?" I asked.

"Oy! My hands are swollen so badly I can hardly move them anymore," she announced.

"I'm sorry to hear that," I said genuinely concerned.

My Auntie Olga doesn't complain readily.

"Ack! What can you do?" she retorted and went back to peeling carrots.

I looked at my sister who was sitting on a chair by the table and avoiding helping as much as she could as usual. I smiled at her and she held up her drink and with a knowing twinkle in her eye and said, "Cheers Seestah!"

I snickered and shook my head. I went up to my Baba and put my arms around her lovely round waist and gave her a kiss on her equally as round, red cheek.

"Hello Baba."

"Oh Hawlo Donia," she said as she gave me a big hug back.

I don't know why, but that hug made me feel like everything was going to be okay. I suddenly felt a peace inside me I hadn't felt in quite some time, which was amazing considering I was in a kitchen full of Ukrainian women! Baba was chopping a mound of onions while my mom was boiling perogies. My Auntie Olga was setting the massive table for twenty eight people. It was so long it went into the living room. My Auntie Rose was cutting the turkey and Auntie Katherine was checking the cabbage rolls. My cousins Shelley, Katrina, Patti and Berni were also helping out. It was harmonic chaos!!!

They were all arguing with each other about how things should be done and how the other person wasn't doing their job correctly. It was a lot of, "No, no, cut the onions smaller Mom!" or "Slice the turkey at an angle!" or "You need to add more water to the cabbage rolls!" The sound between the kitchen and living room was exasperatingly loud. I really wanted to sit and relax, but, under the circumstances, I knew I'd never hear the end of it if I didn't do my share of helping. When I was younger, I was more like my sister, trying to get away with not helping by saying I was tired. That is NOT an excuse when it comes to Ukrainian women. They'd say, "TIRED? I used to get up at 4:30 in the morning when I was nine months pregnant to milk and feed the cows. Then I'd make breakfast for all ten of my children and send them to school. Then I'd clean the house with two babies on my hip. Then I'd..."

It was always that story or some variation of it, and really, what could I say? That's a load of crap? Because it wasn't a load of crap. Those women have worked hard all their lives, and I had no right to complain. Therefore, I learned to stop being lazy and help out, and, in the process, I learned how to make perogies, and how to freeze them properly, which cabbage leaves are the best for making cabbage rolls, and how to make really good borscht. All things I'm happy to know now even if I hated doing it.

"What do you need help with?" I asked.

"You could help me set the table," Auntie Olga replied.

"She should be sitting and relaxing," Auntie Rose countered.

I loved my Aunt Rose. She was my one aunt who didn't take the business of being a baba quite so seriously as the rest.

"No! No! I'm fine," I said begrudgingly.

I looked at the cumbersome table and saw it was missing some cups. I went to the cupboard and reached up to grab a couple when all of a sudden I heard my baba yell, "NOOO!!! NO! NO!"

I was so startled that I just about dropped the cups on my head! I spun (oops!) around to see what tragic set of circumstances could have precipitated such an outburst, thinking maybe Baba had cut off her finger or burned her hand on the stove. When I looked at her she was staring straight at me and shaking her head visibly upset. Everyone was asking her what was wrong.

"What happened Baba?" I asked.

"Never reach for anytheeng above your head," she scolded.

I was confused at why she was telling me this for a few seconds, and then I realized it was obviously another superstition. In that moment, all my stress from the last few months burst out of me.

"WHAT THE HELL ARE YOU TALKING ABOUT?" I yelled loudly enough that a couple of the men actually ventured into the kitchen.

I think Baba was taken aback by my anger. To be honest, so was I. I had NEVER yelled at my baba before. Mind you I had never been that frustrated with her before either. Neither of us said anything for a second.

Then, without warning, a second outburst manifested itself, "SERIOUSLY WHAT ARE YOU TALKING ABOUT? WHAT?!"

Silence. That was probably the quietest that house has ever been.

Finally, my Mom rescued my baba and told me, "It's believed that if you raise your hands above your head, it will cause the umbilical cord to wrap around the baby's neck."

I struggled not to yell again, "Oh for God's sake, that's stupid!" I put the cups down and added in the most immature voice imaginable, "Fine I won't help then!" and stomped into the living room where all the men were avoiding looking at me.

I sat down on the couch and sulked.

I could hear my Mom saying to my Baba, "Don't be too upset with her. It's hormones. She's probably just hungry. You know how crazy some women get when they're pregnant. Remember Jean?"

It was at that moment I felt tremendously horrible, both physically and emotionally. It was like someone had thrown a brick at my chest. I could feel the tears well up, so I got up and ran to the bathroom. After a few minutes, I could hear a light knocking.

"What is it?" was all I could muster up.

"It's me," my mom spoke.

I sighed, knowing I was about to hear it from her.

"Open the door," she said in a voice that I knew meant she wasn't leaving.

I unlocked the door and as soon as I looked at her I burst into tears. For once, I didn't hear lectures. Instead, she just put her arms around me and gave me a hug and let me cry.

Finally, she spoke, "What's wrong?"

"I don't know!" I started crying again, "She's making me crazy with these superstitions and now I'm worried all the time! And even though I don't actually believe any of it, I can hardly do anything without wondering if I'm harming the baby in some way!"

My mother gently and wisely just asked, "Can't you just ignore it?"

I looked at her and shook my head.

"You know she is just trying to be helpful," she continued, "These women are from a different generation than you and these are the things they grew up believing because they were never taught any different. And really who's to say this is true and this isn't true? But by yelling at Baba, you are showing her a disrespect for what SHE holds to be true."

I let this sink in and we just stood silently for a few moments. Then with a sigh I lamented, "Everybody probably hates me now."

"No, no, it's fine!" my mom said unconvincingly, "Come and eat. Fix yourself up though, you look terrible."

Thanks mom!

My mom left and a moment later I heard more knocking.

"I'm coming!" I announced annoyed by my mother's impatience.

"It's me," said Josh.

I opened the door and gave him a sheepish smile, "Told you we shouldn't have come."

"You okay?" he asked.

"Oh lovely," I retorted as I was sniffling and trying to breath through my stuffed nose.

"Well...," he paused, "It was getting too loud in there anyway!"

I laughed. Josh always knew how to make me feel better and he never judged me, even when I was being a total cow, which was the thing I loved about him the most.

"Lets go!"

He grabbed me by the hand as I did the walk of shame to the kitchen table. It was still unusually quiet and I knew it was because of me. I also knew I had to do something about it, so with much embarrassment I did what I had to do.

"I just wanted to tell everyone that I'm very...very sorry I acted in such a bad way."

Silence.

"I also wanted to apologize to Baba for yelling at her," I could feel the tears well up again and couldn't go on.

My Auntie Rose brought me a tissue and patted me on the shoulder.

"I think I'm just feeling tired from being pregnant and...I'm um...hungry," I finished.

Well that was something all Ukrainian's understood - food and eating!

So with that my Uncle Orest bellowed, "Well time to eat then! Smachnoho!"

Everyone shuffled about trying to find a place to sit. I walked by my baba not knowing if I should say something else, so I just grabbed her hand and gave it a squeeze. She took her other hand and patted mine and smiled, but I could see I really hurt her feelings. I felt the tears coming once again, but I took a deep breath and managed to suppress them.

After what was probably ten minutes of confusion and arguing, everyone found a place to sit. My Uncle Tony said a prayer and we began to eat. Twenty eight people, which included Baba, my parents, my sister, my Aunties Olga, Rose and Katherine, my Uncles Orest, Tony and Nestor, my cousins Berni, Patty, Shelley, Katrina, Gerry, Eddie, Garry, and Glen, their kids (who luckily were all downstairs during my outburst) Stephen, Katie, Jordan, Toni, Samantha, Terra-Lynn, Nicole and Ashley, and of course, Josh and me.

Twenty eight people at a table all talking at once made it hard to hear anything anyone said besides the people right next to you, which, luckily, was Josh and my sister who leaned over and whispered drunkenly in my ear,
"Best...Thanksgiving...EVER!"

Don't Go On Any Ships

A week after the Thanksgiving fiasco, as it was aptly named by Josh, I was having lunch with the girls at Tabemasu Sushi, a great Japanese restaurant in town, and regaling them with, admittedly, MY version of the Thanksgiving weekend. For maximum consolation, I put a little less emphasis on my bad behaviour.

Angie, never one to doddle around a subject, exclaimed, "Good grief! What the hell is wrong with your family?"

"With the old country belief system, anything that couldn't be explained practically was given some sort of supernatural explanation. It's very common among Eastern Europeans and many other countries around the world as well," Linda explained to us.

We all looked at her with surprise. Linda wasn't prone to sounding like she was reading from a university textbook. Not to say she wasn't smart. It just wasn't how she spoke.

"Well okay Miss Smarty Pants!" Angie teased her, "That doesn't really explain her parents being that way since they were born in this country."

"We all inherit some of our parent's idiosyncrasies despite our best intentions not to sometimes," she answered again.

We all looked at her again. She obviously needed to explain herself.

"Okay what's up?" Melissa asked.

Linda laughed and explained, "I'm taking an online course on how to improve your vocabulary and grammar. I have a degree for chrissakes and half the time I sound like I work at some hoochie coochie bar."

We all cracked up. That's the Linda we know.

"Well it's working!" I admitted.

At that moment, I heard the shrill tones of my phone ringing out loud.

"Sheesh! Turn that down!" Sandy complained.

I sheepishly apologized and saw that it was my mother calling. I turned my cell on as quickly as I could, because I could see other people were starting to glare at me and my crazy, loud phone. I had a little sigh and rolled up my eyes a bit to my friends and they immediately knew who was calling.

"Hello," I said trying to sound not too unfriendly.

"I just wanted to know if you're still coming tomorrow?"

My mother doesn't usually beat around the bush either.

"Coming where?" I asked, genuinely not having a clue.

"To Babas! Don't you remember? We're going to be making perogies for Christmas!" she snapped.

I groaned. That was the LAST thing I wanted to do.

"Why do we need to make perogies this early!" I complained.

It was at that moment one of the waiters dropped a plate a few tables down from us.

"Where are you?" my mother demanded to know.

"Having lunch with the girls," I told her.

"Well anyway, you're coming?" I had a distinct feeling it wasn't a choice.

"I don't know if it's such a good idea after last week," I said smiling knowingly at the girls.

My mother had had enough.

"LOOK!" she barked, "Baba was very hurt by what you said and you need to make things right with her!"

I was taken aback by her harshness and I immediately felt uncomfortable.

I simply said, "Fine."

"Okay we'll go after church," she told me and I agreed not wanting to be yelled at again.

She hung up on me. Great!

"Guess where I get to go tomorrow?" I asked in my best faux enthusiastic voice.

"It's probably best to make amends with your baba," Melissa said.

"Yes I know," I muttered. "It's just always so aggravating. I never know what's going to come out of her mouth and the last thing I need is more stress. Dr. Rens told me that I better start taking it easy."

"How is Robin these days?" Angie mischievously asked.

They had all been to Dr. Rens at one time or another and they all knew I was harbouring a bit of a crush on him as well. I was pretty sure I wasn't the only one.

"He's fine," I said nonchalantly as possible. "Like I said, he's worried about my stress levels. He says if I don't relax, I'll end up on bed rest."

"Well cut it out then!" Linda poked me in the arm and smiled.

"ACTUALLY...," I paused for dramatic emphasis, "Josh has been worried about me too and he's decided that we should go on a little vacay during the Christmas break."

"I hate you!" Linda retorted in mock jealousy, "Must be nice to have some nice, rich lawyer to take you to all these great places."

"Oh it is!!!" I teased her back.

"Where are you going?" Melissa asked.

"We're thinking of a Caribbean cruise," I replied, "But we're not one hundred percent sure yet.

Actually, I'm going to the travel agency after lunch to see what our options are."

"Well let me know," Angie said, "Rich and I are possibly planning a trip around then too. Maybe we can go with you guys!"

"Awesome!" I replied, although I wasn't sure if Josh would be on board with that idea. He wasn't exactly the biggest fan of Angie's husband. The guy is a bit boorish. Honestly, I wasn't sure what she saw in him. Not that I'd ever tell her that. She was pretty defensive when it came to him. I figured Josh didn't need to know right away since nothing was set in stone anyway.

The rest of lunch went by quickly and when it was done, I made my way to the travel agency excited about the prospect of getting away for the holidays.

When I got home, I immediately phoned Deanna and made plans to meet with her and the rest of the girls the next day. I figured I would need a get away plan in place. She was super excited and, truth be told, so was I.

I didn't get to spend a lot of time with my Ituna friends anymore. Admittedly, I had, on more than one occasion, cancelled outings with my Ituna friends to do something with my Yorkton friends.

It wasn't necessarily that I liked one set of friends more than the other, but with my Yorkton friends, the conversation was always a bit more interesting and livelier. On the other hand, sometimes there's nothing like old friends.

Josh came home from doing some work at the office and we went through the brochures I picked up at the travel agency while I made supper. We narrowed it down to either a Caribbean or Bahamas cruise. I was super excited! "This is exactly what I need," I kept thinking to myself.

The next morning was overcast and I fought the urge of feeling grey myself. The plan was that Josh and I would go to church and, after church was done, I would just go with my mom and Josh would take my dad home. I wanted to drive, but my mom insisted that she was driving and tried to tell me that my driving scared her. She should talk! While I do admit my driving skills have been, in the past, questionable, she certainly isn't much better herself. She never pays attention when she's driving. She once ran into a Mercedes in the middle of a Walmart parking lot right after I told her to watch where she was going. Luckily, she just caught the corner and really only cracked the plastic that covered the signal light. However, it cost $500 and that was 20 years ago! The point is she was always getting into these little fender benders, while my driving record had been great for the last five years. I do have an issue with road rage though. I once honked the horn and started yelling at an old man because he took our parking spot...while my mom was driving!

Not wanting to start off with an argument, I agreed to let her drive even if it made me feel a bit like a prisoner.

When we got into her car, the first thing she said to me was, "What are you wearing?"

Typical! I was wearing leggings and sweater with big, winter boots. They were definitely not my Sunday best and definitely not acceptable church clothes according to my mother.

"What does it matter?" I bitched, "All my clothes are getting too tight and, besides, I wasn't going to wear anything fancy to make perogies."

"You could have brought a change of clothes," she countered.

"Mom only old people dress up for church now," I knew this would sting as she was always "to the nines" on Sunday mornings.

"Hmph!" was her only reply.

Just to irk her some more, I added, "Oh by the way, I'm going for coffee with the girls at 3:30.

"Emma!" she growled at me.

"What?" I growled back.

She just shook her head and grumbled, "Well let's get going then, so you can make at least a couple of perogies."

I snorted to myself. Both her and I knew well enough that my baba would have been up since five this morning and would have everything ready to go by the time we got there. She may even already be half done. My baba didn't wait for anyone!!

As we drove off, my mother mentioned that she had brought sandwiches and fruit for the trip. I was incredibly grateful since I was starving, so I delved right in and grabbed a tuna sandwich. We spent the rest of the trip with her babbling away about how my sister is irresponsible, how the ladies in the women's church league are lazy, how my father still hasn't painted the downstairs bathroom and on and on. I just let her vent, while I snarfed down the food. I was in a constant state of hunger these days, so I was happy to let her chatter away while I stuffed my face.

I felt fine until I saw the familiar signs that meant we were approaching town. I felt my stomach starting to twist and tense up. I tried to think of other things, but nothing worked. By the time we got to Baba's house, I was really feeling sick and felt like I was going to vomit. As soon as my mother stopped the car, I ran to the back of the house, but stopped short of going in realizing I wouldn't make it. Luckily, there was an empty bucket Baba used for carrying vegetables from her garden and did my business in there.

My mother took forever, but finally sauntered up beside me, my head still in the bucket. I was heaving and gasping for air. Instead of asking me if I was okay, she felt it necessary to tell Mr. Blazieko next door, who had witnessed the whole thing, that it was morning sickness. Then, she turned to me and just shook her head. She went inside and I took a minute to compose myself while Mr. Blazieko, the creepy old bugger that he is, stared at me without saying a word.

Deciding that this whole incident was probably some sort of bad omen and indicative of how my visit with Baba would be, I felt a surge of bitchiness overcoming me, so as I was opening the door to Baba's house I glared at Mr. Blazieko and snarled, "I'm FINE! Thanks for asking!"

When I stepped into the house and walked up the three steps that led into the kitchen, it was like stepping into a war zone. Mass pandemonium, complete with loud talking (because is there really any other kind with Ukrainians?), running around and mountains of food. These ladies were already in full swing. The sight of all those women brought me back to Thanksgiving and I felt another surge of sickness starting to rise. I sat down and put my head down hoping that would help. In the midst of all this, my Baba brought me some soup and quickly placed it in front of me. Actually, she practically threw it and raced back to the dough.

It reminded me of when Josh and I went to Paris for our first anniversary and we found this quaint Parisienne cafe complete with a snooty waiter. He threw our plates of steak frites in the exact same manner as Baba, with the perfect amount of disdain and haughtiness you'd expect from a French waiter. We were thrilled to get the full French experience. However, with Baba, not so much. I could tell Baba was not happy with me. I could tell no one was comfortable because even in the midst of the chaos, there was an odd sort of tension.

I sat there, not knowing what to do, until finally my baba turned to look at me and demanded, "Eat! EAT!"

"Not sure I can Baba!" I replied trying to be as pleasant as possible.

"Chomu? Why?" Baba asked me concerned.

"Morning sickness," my mother randomly called out again, despite knowing full well that everyone knew it was a lie.

"My stomach isn't good," I admitted and as I looked up at Baba and her crinkly blue eyes, I could feel my own eyes getting watery.

I wasn't surprised. I was currently crying at least once a day, mostly at stupid things, like insurance commercials or Hallmark cards. However, this time, I genuinely felt terrible as the stress of the last couple of months was starting to take their toll. My baba patted me on my head sweetly and I stood up and hugged her doughy frame. When I let go, she told me to hold on and she went into her "special" cupboard. The one filled with herbs and spices, among other things, that she used as a Babky. She grabbed a few things and went and mixed a few ingredients together, added some water and gave it to me.

"Drink!" she ordered.

I took a sniff.

"What is it?" I asked.

Besides some ginger, I had no idea.

"DRINK!" she ordered again.

I knew I had no choice, so I took a little sip at first to test the concoction out. Along with the ginger, I could definitely taste licorice as well, and something else that was familiar, but I couldn't quite make it out. It wasn't particularly appetizing, but not awful either, so down the hatch it went.

"Day Bozhe!" I joked and everyone laughed.

After that, the atmosphere eased up considerably and we spent the next few hours making the delicious, little dumplings that were going to grace the table at Christmas.

At around 3:30, Deanna called and asked if I was ready to go. I was actually having a great time with my baba, aunts and mom. They were telling me stories about the "good ole days" before thing got "crazy with the terrorists and internet and all that!" Additionally, I knew that I'd get to eat some of the perogies if I stayed at Baba's. Not that I hadn't been tasting them here and there already. However, I had promised the girls and knew I should go.

I hadn't seen most of them since before announcing my pregnancy and they were all really excited to talk about it. I wasn't sure why since they all had been pregnant at least twice each themselves, but I just chalked it up to living in a small town where even the smallest of news like the church getting new carpet, makes the local paper.

I told Deanna I'd meet them in ten minutes at Ituna's Country Cafe.

When I got off the phone, my mom asked who I was speaking too like she didn't know already.

I sighed and shook my head at her, but I answered, "Deanna."

"So you're going to leave then?" she announced loud enough for most of the town to hear.

"I already mentioned this to you Mother!!" I said in mock sweetness that was meant to tell her to lay off.

"Why don't you have something to eat first?" my Auntie Olga asked.

"Would love to, really, but we're going to the cafe, so I'm sure I'll grab something there," I replied.

"ICK! A fattening hamburger and greasy fries?" my mother asked indignantly.

"Yummy!" I licked my lips and rubbed my stomach just to annoy her.

But she knew how to get back at me.

"You know you better watch what you're eating, you don't want to put on too much weight. How much have you gained so far?" she asked with mock sincerity.

I swear sometimes she just likes to pick a fight with me, because she knows my weight is a sensitive issue, even though I pretend it's not. To make things worse, Dr. Rens had just warned me that about gaining too much weight.

"I'm FINE!" I remarked a little too forcefully.

"I'm just saying," my mother replied in the smug way that she does sometimes that makes me want to punch her in the face.

Yeah I know, that's a terrible thing to say, but, as I said, my mother is just one of those people who can make me want to commit violence.

Suddenly, I couldn't wait to leave, so I pointed out to my mother, "Look! I haven't seen the girls in

MONTHS and they all want to have a nice visit with me and talk about my pregnancy and catch up. If I don't do it now, who knows when we'll all be able to get together again?"

"What about Christmas?" my mom asked.

Oh here we go! I had wanted to avoid mentioning the cruise to my mother, because I knew she'd make me feel guilty about going by saying things like we should spend time with the family, because everyone is getting older and, "Well you just never know how much longer they'll be with us!" We missed Easter once to go visit friends in Calgary and I still hear about it at least once a month, and that was FOUR years ago!

"Well," I paused, figuring out how to break it to her, "actually...we're planning to go on a Caribbean cruise."

I tensed up, getting prepared for the inevitable backlash. What came next wasn't quite expected, well, on second thought, maybe it was.

"NOOOO!!" Baba cried out.

Everyone's heads turned towards Baba.

"What's wrong Mom?" my mom asked worriedly.

Baba was looking straight at me. All of a sudden, I got a sense of deja vu and knew what was coming. It was Thanksgiving all over again.

"You can't go on NO sheeps!" my Baba announced quite matter-of-factly.

I had no idea of what to say for a minute. I even looked at my aunts and mom for an explanation, but they seemed as lost as I was.

Finally, I asked, "Why Baba?"

She answered with her rote response, "Ees bad!"

However, I wasn't accepting "ees bad" anymore, as if that was all that was needed as an explanation.

"Chomu?" I asked again.

She looked reluctant to say anything at first, but finally blurted out, "Ees bad luck to go on sheeps when you're praygrent."

My Baba says praygrent and not pregnant and getting her to say it correctly is a near impossibility.

My reaction was, unfortunately, typical. I foolishly thought for a minute that this afternoon had actually erased all the craziness of the previous months, but my frustration came back in one fell swoop and, to be honest, a terrible sense of disappointment had just washed over me like a tidal wave.

"JESUS BABA!" I whined loudly.

My Auntie Katherine crossed herself.

"EMMA!" my mom used her warning voice that let me to know she would not tolerate any crap from me.

I usually didn't heed the warning voice, but today was an exception. I knew what it could turn into all too well and I simply just did not want to go there again. However, I couldn't really just let it go either, so while suppressing my urge to let out a primal scream, I just said, "That's silly! It will be fine!"

Apparently, that wasn't good enough though, "No no! You DON'T go on sheeps when you are praygrent! Wery, wery bad luck!" she insisted.

I had enough, "What's going to happen? Is the baby going to look like a dolphin because we've been on the ocean?" I inquired sarcastically.

The look on Baba's face told me that I had gone too far. I attempted to brush it off as a joke and make light of it all, "Oh Baba! You worry too much!"

I feebly laughed and gave her a quick hug and kiss on her flushed, round cheek, but I could feel her tensing up as I did.

I knew I needed to get out quickly before I cause any more damage, so I grabbed my purse and started out the kitchen door, "I'll see you ladies later," I called out cheerily trying to lighten the mood.

I could see my mother scowling at me though, and that was the last thing I saw as I left the house. As soon as I stepped outside, I felt that familiar feeling again and rushed to the bucket. Dammit anyway!

I walked to the Country Cafe, or "the cuh-fay", as the locals pronounced it. It was a very typical small town cafe with John Deere posters and a photo of the aerial view of the owner's old farm on the walls. I think every farmer in the area had one hanging on his wall.

The walk only took me a few minutes, but thankfully, it was enough to clear my head. Walking into the cafe and seeing all my old friends gave me a much needed lift of spirit.

"Hey ladies!" I called out warmly and proceeded to give them all big hugs, something that, for some reason, I didn't feel comfortable doing with my city friends. With them, it was usually the more European inspired kiss on the cheek greeting, which would garner quite a lot of gossip if I were to attempt it in Ituna.

"So how are you guys?" I asked warmly.

"More importantly," Kay, who had five children, asked, "How are YOU?"

I was about to go into the usual pregnancy diatribe of my clothes not fitting, my unusual craving for Gatorade and so forth, but, without a thought, I went instead into my whole Baba dilemma. When I finished with the latest "bout of ridiculousness", I got a round of laughter.

"Oh honey!" my friend Barb, who was quite a drama queen herself, empathized, "My baba babysits for me three days a week when I'm at work and Starla comes home with the CRAZIEST things!!! It really is enough to make you INSANE!! I totally hear ya!"

"I KNOW!" I yelled out in utter agreement.

A few old farmers out for their Sunday afternoon coffee turned and looked at us disapprovingly. We all giggled. It felt so good to unleash all my frustration to people who truly understood what I was going through. I decided to keep going and went on about the Thanksgiving fiasco having left it out before just in case my woes didn't fall on sympathetic ears. I should have stopped while the going was good though, because the Thanksgiving story did NOT get the same response.

There was silence and then, "Oh...what did your mom say?" Deanna asked.

I felt like saying I didn't really give a damn what my mom thought, but thought I had better not, especially since it wasn't technically true.

"Well, she wasn't too happy with me obviously, and I felt really bad of course and apologized immediately," I answered trying to make myself not look like this terrible person who yells at her poor, little old grandmother. Although, as much as I didn't want to admit it, that's exactly what I was.

"Well pregnancy hormones will make you do crazy things sometimes," Kay offered nicely.

The others nodded in what seemed like reluctant agreement. I sat there feeling like a total jerk. Desperate to change the conversation, I asked them about how the crops did this year, even though I could honestly care less about the crops, but anything was better than the uncomfortable silence.

Luckily, that seemed to do the trick and the girls waxed on for the next hour about farming problems, the weather, and the church. Same old, same old. I sat and tried to talk as little as possible and was incredibly thankful when my cell phone rang and my mom told me it was time to go.

I said good bye to the girls and gave them all another hug, but, like Baba's, they weren't as warm as the first ones, with the exception of Deanna's. She gave me a smile and a wink that told me she didn't judge me. I felt a little better and smiled back. I waved to everyone as I prepared to walk back to Baba's, but my mother was in front of the cafe with her car running.

"What are you doing?" I asked, "I could have walked back."

All she said was, "This will save time."

"But I wanted to say goodbye to Baba and the aunties," I insisted.

"Baba went for a nap," my mother said tersely.

"Oh," I replied quietly, "Must be tired from all the cooking," I offered.

"Hm," was all my mom replied back.

The whole drive home was silent and even though I hated to admit it, I knew I had screwed up again.

Don't Buy Anything for the Baby

The couple weeks after our trip to Ituna were strange. I had only spoken to my mother once in those two weeks and I usually spoke to her two or three times a day. As well, my daily calls from Baba had stopped. I felt an odd sense of forlornness during this time and I couldn't help but think it was all my fault, which didn't help to improve my mood.

The situation at work only added to the overall mayhem that was my life during this point. Mr. Morales, the zealous, evil jerk that he was, had decided to make it his mission to make my life a living hell every opportunity he could get. Thank GOD for Cindy and Janie, or I most certainly would have quit. I came close several times. It was like he had this sixth sense that my stress levels had almost reached their peak and he was making it his own personal mission to make sure I would reach full insanity.

All teachers at our school were required to supervise extra-curricular activities during the year. Most teachers had picked their activities and very little changed from year to year. I had expected that I would be doing the same thing as the last few years. This included lunch supervision twice a week, supervising school dances, being in charge of ticket sales and publicity for the school drama productions and being the teacher rep for the Student Council. All in all, I didn't mind doing any of these things because they didn't require a lot of personal time from me, unlike, for instance, the football coaches or the teachers that helped run the school newspaper. However, this year Morales had decided that my involvement in the school wasn't satisfactory. It wasn't enough that he had to torture me with Gr. 10 English, for which he had never found a replacement, but he decided that I should be the supervisor for the poetry club as well.

"We have a poetry club?" I asked, only half joking.

I had, oddly enough, never heard about it before. He looked at me over his bifocals as if I were an idiot, sighed and shook his head.

"Yes!" he answered back unamused, "They meet Wednesday's at lunch in the library."

FUN!!!

"Okay then!" I replied with the biggest, fakest smile I could muster.

I absolutely needed to show that man he couldn't break me. He wasn't, however, done with me yet, "Oh and I need you to coach the badminton team."

"The what???" I asked confused.

I couldn't, for the life of me, fathom why he'd ask me to do that, because no one in their right mind would ever ask me to coach a sports team, especially for a sport I had never played and knew nothing about.

"Mrs. Lekach coached the team, but now that she has retired, they need a coach and that will be you. They will be meeting Tuesday and Thursday mornings before school."

At that moment, it took every ounce of energy I had, not to lean over and strangle his neck. That's when I saw it. The smile. I realized, and even worse, he realized, that he had gotten the best of me. There was no sense in arguing with him that I had no idea how to play badminton or that I wasn't much of a morning person or even that my doctor had ordered me to ease up on my activities, because he simply did not care.

"Fine!" was my answer and I got up without another word and walked out before the jerk could see me cry.

I immediately found Cindy and Janie and mentioned that we needed to have a TR meeting tout de suite. TR stands for Teacher's Rage. We invented it when Morales became our principal. With his ridiculous demands and dour personality, it was the only way we kept our sanity.

We'd meet in the Drama storage room where they kept costumes, props, staging and all things theatrical, because it was private and there was no chance of a student popping in unexpectedly since they always needed permission to go into that room. We kept a secret stash of vodka hidden away behind some old costumes. It was like our way of saying "screw you" to the tyranny of John Morales and his dictatorial rules.

Five minutes later, we were huddled around stacks of scripts, fake swords, masks, and theatre paraphernalia and I was vocalizing, in top form, my anger about what had just happened. Cindy and Janie drank from the tiny, silver flask of vodka, something I was very sad that I couldn't also participate in, as they nodded their heads in complete empathy. By the time the bell rang, we had agreed that John Morales was evil incarnate and probably possessed by the devil himself. Needless to say, I felt much better.

When I got home, there was a message from my mother on the answering machine. It was something about how she forgot to give me some tea Baba had made for me when we were in Ituna. I was busy opening the mail when I was listening to the message so I didn't quite get everything she had said. I decided to just call her back.

"Hey!" I said cheerfully hoping to ease up the mood straight away.

"Oh hi!" she replied sounding distracted.

"What's up?" I asked.

"What do you mean?" she responded.

What did she think I meant?

"How's it going?" I clarified.

"Oh fine!"

That was it. Nothing else. I knew things were bad when my mom didn't want to talk to me. I decided that I needed to try to make peace, but wasn't sure how to go about it when an idea hit me.

"So hey," I started, "All my clothes are WAY too tight on me. Would you like to go maternity clothes shopping with me on Saturday?"

She paused for a second, like she was thinking about it and then warmly said, "Sure!"

I added cheerfully, "Maybe we could look for some stuff for the baby too."

She didn't say anything.

"Mom?" I called out thinking maybe she wasn't there.

"Yeah I'm here," she answered.

"Why didn't you answer then?" I asked.

She hesitated for a moment then responded, "I'm sure you won't want to hear it."

This didn't sound good, but I was curious to know what was on her mind.

"No tell me!" I demanded.

She didn't answer right away and when she did, she said it quickly and to the point, "Baba said to not buy anything for the baby before it's born."

It was my turn to be silent, but I could feel myself tensing up.

I wasn't going there. I just couldn't, so I simply said, "Well I guess we won't do that then."

She seemed quite relieved that I didn't make a big issue about it, but I have to say I wasn't.

"I have to go now," was all I could muster up.

"Okay!" she chirped and then added, "Oh and I'll bring that tea that Baba made you on Saturday."

"What's it for anyway?" I grumbled.

"Morning sickness," she replied without a hint of the ridiculousness of her answer.

"But I don...," I started, but then changed my mind and stopped. I took a deep breath and said, "Okay then."

I got off the phone and looked around for something to hit. I felt tears stinging my eyes. What the HELL is wrong with me?

I was SO sick of crying. I was even more sick of feeling angry and worried all the time, but I couldn't seem to help myself. What was worse was that I couldn't decide if it was a symptom of being pregnant, or if I was just simply the world's biggest bitch and hadn't realized it until now. Would I be like this if I didn't have Baba constantly on my back, or would it just be something else that would bother me? I contemplated this while I made supper for myself. Unfortunately, Josh would be home late again. Along with a few big cases he had been assigned, his dad insisted that Josh start bringing in new clientele. This meant some late nights schmoozing potential clients. I was frustrated because my lower back was killing me and I just wanted him home to listen and make me feel better. However, since that wasn't going to happen, I took a nice warm bubble bath and put on some music and felt much better.

By the time I got out of the bath, I was actually smiling. I put on this old red Gap shirt I used as pajamas. It had a bunch of big holes and a green splotch of paint across the left breast area - a reminder from a crazy, Picasso inspired evening when I stayed up until three in the morning trying my hand at Cubism. Despite its raucous appearance, I loved the shirt. It was incredibly comfortable and wearing it relaxed me.

I had decided to go to bed early hoping that this would mean I would rise early to make it to badminton practice on time. I pulled out a book I had gotten at the library on how to play badminton, since I didn't want to seem like a complete moron at the practice tomorrow. I had just sat down on my bed after putting two pillows behind me and pulling my silvery grey comforter up to my chest when the phone rang. I grumbled, not really wanting to get up and chiding myself for not thinking of putting the phone beside me, since the phone was on Josh's side of the bed. I moved over and reached around the side table and picked up the phone. For a second I had this terrible thought that maybe something bad had happened to Josh, and my over active imagination pictured having to go on with life as a single mother. I snapped out of it quickly when the phone rang for the fourth time. I knew that if I didn't pick it up right away, the answering machine would come on, so I quickly checked the name and saw that it was Deanna.

"Weird," I thought to myself.

She never called past seven. I immediately became worried again and pressed the talk button on the phone quickly.

"Hi!" I said too loudly.

"Hi," she answered back in an almost inaudible whisper.

I realized her kids were probably sleeping, which would explain the hushed voice.

"What's up?" I asked.

"Sorry for calling so late," she replied again with a muted tone.

I looked at the clock. It was not even ten yet! I laughed.

"No biggie!" I replied, "It's still early for me, although I am in bed for once."

"Oooh sorry!" she moaned.

"No no! I wasn't sleeping," I reassured her, "Just reading about badminton in bed. My dumb ass principal thought it would be a good idea for me to coach the badminton team of all things, and they have their practices at seven in the morning if you can imagine."

"Hmm no," she murmured.

I got the distinct feeling she wasn't all that interested in what I had to say. I figured I should roll the conversation back her way.

"So what's the sitch bitch?" I asked uttering the phrase my Yorkton friends and I sometimes used.

"What?" she sounded alarmed and confused.

"Oh nothing, nothing!" I felt embarrassed and a bit flustered all of a sudden, "It's just something I say sometimes," I remarked trying to make light of the "sitch", "Why are you calling?" I rephrased.

"Oh!" she responded, "I could only call when Derrick was asleep."

Derrick was Deanna's husband. While he was your stereotypical farm boy who liked to talk about his crops pretty much all the time, he was a lot of fun and I liked him a lot. He always treated Deanna really well and was a really great father to their kids. He also had the most patience I have ever seen in a person.

Deanna kept going, "It's his thirtieth birthday coming up next Friday and we're having a surprise birthday for him."

"Oh," I paused, and then said, "Cool!" for lack of a better answer.

Deanna didn't say anything for a few seconds and I didn't really know what else to say.

Finally, she asked, "Well...can you come?"

"Ooooh," I laughed realizing what she was waiting for, "Um the 20th? I think that should be fine, I'll have to check with Josh. Things have been really crazy for him at work lately, but I'm sure it will be fine," I answered, "He'll be excited to come!" I added.

However, I wasn't completely sure about that. Josh wasn't what you'd call the most sociable of people, especially around my friends for some reason. He would often find some quiet corner at their parties and sit by himself. He would only speak to someone if they spoke to him first. I often felt embarrassed by his seemingly rude behaviour and wished he made more of an effort. Time and time again, I begged him to make more of an effort. Josh didn't have a lot of friends to begin with, and the few close friends that he did have, lived far away. His best friend Tom lived in California of all places, where he practiced entertainment law. He was married to a former playboy bunny named Celia. I wanted to not like her for obvious reasons, but it turned out that she was really sweet and we've become great friends as well.

"Anyway," I continued, "I'll call you back tomorrow and let you know for sure."

"Okay," she answered breezily.

There was a pause again and I got the feeling she was wanting to talk some more, but I was pretty tired from the warm bath and I still needed to read my badminton book, so I said goodbye and hung up the phone. Sighing, I opened up my book and within three minutes I was fast asleep.

Three days later, it was Saturday and I was preparing for my shopping day with my mom. Josh had gone to the office an hour earlier, because he promised he'd be home early for once. He was actually going to take me out for dinner and possibly even a movie if I was up for it.

When I was ready to go, I called my mom, "Hey are you ready to go?" We decided a day earlier that I would drive.

I could hear my dad yelling in the background as she spoke, "I'm helping your dad put bookshelves together."

Not exactly the answer I was looking for, but, knowing how my dad got when he was doing any type of manual labour that involved instructions, I knew she wouldn't be able to leave until they were done.

"Well how long is that going to take?" I asked.

I had little to no patience of any kind, so it was generally hard for me to wait for anyone.

"Oh it shouldn't be much longer," she answered.

Then I heard my dad yelling again, "Who are you talking to? Get off the bloody phone!!!"

I sighed, but wasn't really surprised. My dad was cranky about fifty percent of the time, and when he is stressed out, it was one hundred percent of the time. I don't know how my mom stands it to be honest. Mind you, it has been pointed out, on more than one occasion, that I'm exactly like him. Of course, I always disagree with that misguided assessment of my personality, but, unfortunately, you can't always change people's minds. In any event, I didn't really feel like listening about how my mother can't hold a board straight or whatever his problem was with her right now, so I just told her to call back when they were done.

Surprisingly, it was only fifteen minutes later when she called back, "Has the tragedy been solved?" I asked sarcastically.

I often tried to soften my dad's temper with actual facts of tragic circumstances, like children with incurable cancer or the cutting down of the rain forests, in a vain attempt to make him realize his situation was not all that bad and certainly not worth all the commotion. I'm not sure he really appreciated my efforts.

Mom just laughed, as she usually did, which I could never understand. I was often way angrier at him than her.

"Come get me," she said.

"Okay," I answered, "See you in five."

Yorkton doesn't have much in the way of trendy or interesting clothes, and as for maternity clothes, you may as well forget it. I decided to try and go for larger sized clothing instead of actual maternity wear, and, I did, thankfully, manage to find a few things.

When we were done, mom asked if I wanted to go for a drink. I paused for a second before I answered, because while we actually had a pleasant day and she did buy most of my clothes for me, I didn't want to push things. The longer my mom and I hung out, the more likely we were to argue about something. I was trying to avoid any arguments, because I had just read in one of my pregnancy books that the baby could now hear sounds. However, I was dying for a cool drink, so I agreed.

We stopped at the Cup & Saucer, a new coffee shop that had opened up recently and that we both wanted to try. It felt good to sit and relax after all the walking around we had done in the last couple of hours.

As soon as we sat down, she said, "Oh, I almost forgot, here's that tea Baba made for you."

I tensed up for the briefest of seconds, but took a deep breath and managed to relax right back down again.

"Thanks," I managed, "What, exactly, is in it?"

"I don't know!" she answered in a sing songy kind of voice.

Boy she was in a good mood.

"Hm," I answered, but couldn't resist adding, "You do know that I don't have morning sickness, right?"

"Oh I know," she answered, "But Baba said it's also good for the baby and you should drink it all through your pregnancy."

Feeling sarcastic, I joked, "Yeah? Well she also told me that if I ever got frightened by an animal, the baby would end up looking like that animal."

She smiled slightly, but I could tell she wasn't too happy about the remark.

She hesitated for a second and then finally spit out, "Emma... your Baba, she's just trying to...she wants to... she just wants everything to be okay."

"And that is fine," I pointedly answered back, "BUT do you know how frustrating it is to be told all these silly rules to follow about what I can or cannot do or eat or...whatever, because the baby will be birth marked or look like a dog or be short or cranky or stupid or have webbed feet or will turn into a werewolf at midnight when there's a full moon?"

She laughed and teasingly said, "Well how do you know those things won't happen?"

"MOM!" I pleaded, "Advice I can handle, but most of what she tells me is INSANE!"

I was starting to get a little incensed now, "And the crazy thing is that I actually think twice now before I eat red food or cross my legs or look at something ugly for too long."

My mother sighed, "I don't know what to tell you."

"I realize that it's just her way and it's what she believes, I really do, but it's causing me to worry all the time! Can't you tell her to stop?" I asked.

Then I added accusingly, "Tell her that my doctor said it's causing me too much stress and THAT is something that could hurt the baby...and me!"

"Why can't you just be good humoured about all this?" she asked, "You're so much like your dad sometimes."

"I am not!" I fumed.

Seeing that none of the usual tactics were working, she used the one thing all Catholics understand…GUILT!

"You know your Baba is getting older. She might not be around much longer," she warned.

"That woman is probably going to outlive all of us!" I quipped.

"Don't be so sure of that," she replied cryptically.

"Why?" I asked a bit alarmed by her answer, "What's wrong with her?"

"Oh nothing, nothing," she replied a little too quickly, "But you know how her heart is and her blood pressure has been quite high lately."

Her answer gave me pause.

"Have you ever thought," she added, "that she may be stressed out by this situation with you as well?"

Well no Mom, I hadn't realized that at all! Dammit anyway! I hated when she did this because now all I could think about was what if something happened to her. It would be all my fault. Wonderful! Just what I needed to hear!

I was tired of talking about the whole thing, so I changed the subject.

"So guess what?" I piped up after a few contemplative moments, "Deanna is having a surprise thirtieth birthday party for Derrick."

My mom snorted and shook her head her head.

"I don't know how that girl can afford to do anything with all the travelling she does," she responded.

That's my mom for you. Always an unbiased opinion about everything. Deanna often took her kids here and there for lessons, or to shop, or just to see the world. Many people thought she should just stick herself in the kitchen like a good farm wife and feed her husband and kids and never mind about going to all these places.

"MAYBE she just doesn't like to be stuck in a small town with small town people and nothing to do!" I was really aggravated now and feeling somewhat superior at that moment.

"Oh Emma!" my mom said just shaking her head at me in that judgemental way she does all the time.

The annoying thing was that she was giving me grief for acting the very same way she was acting herself. I found this infuriatingly hypocritical.

"Why do you always have to have a negative comment?" I was getting incensed again.

"I'm not negative," was her unsurprisingly reply, because she actually truly does not think she's being negative.

"YES! You are!!" I countered.

She changed the subject this time.

"Are you staying overnight in Ituna?" she asked.

"I don't know," I replied, kind of glad to be talking about something else.

I had only mentioned the party once to Josh and he gave me some half-hearted affirmation that we'd go.

"Well," my mom spoke, interrupting my thoughts, "Make sure you phone Baba and let her know. I don't like you guys driving at night so you really should stay at Baba's. Just let her know," she repeated.

I hated to agree with her, but I didn't particularly like driving at night either, especially during the winter. A close friend of mine, Brenda, came across an accident on the highway one evening a few years back, and the graphic details of the accident still left me feeling uneasy. I made a mental note to mention it to Josh that night.

My mom then started chattering away about my sister and I let her do most of the talking for the rest of the time.

It ended up taking two days for me to gain the courage to call Baba. Josh begrudgingly agreed to stay overnight in Ituna.

"Hawlo?" Baba answered like she wasn't sure what was going on.

"Hi Baba!" I replied cheerfully as possible.

"Oh Hawlo Donia!"

It may have just been me, but I thought I noted a slight tautness in her voice. I thought about what my mom said and tried to remain cheerful.

"Well, first of all, I just wanted to say thank-you for the tea," I started.

Silence.

"The tea Baba," I yelled, "Dyakuyu!"

"Ooooh tak, tak! Yes! You're welcome!" she replied loudly finally hearing what I was saying.

My Baba is pretty deaf, but refuses to get hearing aids, so you often had to repeat yourself.

"Are you dreenking eet EVERY day?" she asked loudly again.

"Tak!" I lied.

I had read that pregnant women shouldn't drink most herbs. I phoned my doctor to ask him about it and he freaked out on me. Sheesh! I really should get myself a new doctor. What is it about good looking men that makes us lose our senses???

"So Baba," I continued to talk before she could say anything else about the tea and I would have to lie to her again.

"Yes?" she answered.

"We are coming to Ituna next Friday for a party at Deanna's house and we were wondering if we could stay overnight at your house?" I asked.

"Oh sure, sure!" she said enthusiastically.

I was so relieved by the response and replied, "Great! Well we'll see you on Friday then okay?"

"Oookay," she replied back and hung up without saying goodbye, which was what she usually did.

I hung up the phone and sat there for a second. A big smile crept up on my face.

Don't Eat Fish

Friday came quickly and Josh and I managed to leave right after school ended, which was amazing because he had been having to work late every day that week. It was a beautiful day, with the pure white snow sparkling in the sunlight making it twinkle like there were millions of diamonds lying scattered on the ground. The hoar frost on the trees was so indescribably picturesque that it could almost take your breath away. Normally I wasn't a big fan of the snow and, more accurately, the piercing cold winters, but the bigger I got, the higher my internal temperature seem to get, and so the coldness of the air actually felt wonderful.

Josh was unusually quiet, even for him, which I would normally find frustrating, because it meant that I couldn't get a word out of him when I wanted to have a conversation. However, it had been a crazy day at school, so I didn't mind the peace and quiet. We just listened to the radio and had a relaxing drive to Ituna.

As we were approaching Ituna, I felt "it"! At first I didn't know what "it" was, but then it happened again.

"Josh!" I said very excitedly, "JOSH!"

"What?" he looked at me worriedly.

"I felt it move! I felt the baby MOVE!"

His eyes got big and a smile appeared, "Really?"

"Oh my God yes!" I was so excited and a little freaked out at the same time.

I grabbed his hand to the place I felt the movement. Then there was...nothing. Eventually Josh decided he needed his hand to drive, but not without promising him that I would let him know next time I felt the baby move.

When we got to Baba's house, the baby had still not moved again. I was disappointed for Josh, but still so excited that I had felt that weird, but wonderful, sensation. Of course Josh had to dissolve my excitement.

As I opened the car door, I noticed he wasn't doing the same thing.

"Why aren't you moving?" I asked.

"Uh," was his response.

"Oh this can't be good!" I thought to myself.

I sat back down and closed the door and gave him my undivided attention.

"Listen," he started, "I've been trying to think of way to tell you this since we left town."

"What?" I inquired not so nicely.

"Well," he paused to clear his throat, "As you know my dad has been getting me to work with him on the Anderson case, which is one of the reasons why I've been working so late lately."

I didn't like where this was going, but I let him continue.

"And he's now decided that I should take it over," he said enthusiastically trying to get me to be on his side, but I wasn't biting.

He paused for a second like the calm before the storm, and then laid the rest on me, "So unfortunately that means we won't be able to go on our trip."

He rushed it all out like he was ripping a band aid off a wound, thinking it would hurt less if he said it quickly. He was wrong!

At first I didn't say anything, because I thought maybe he was joking. When I realized he wasn't, I didn't know how to respond at first, so I said nothing. I think this scared Josh more than anything else. I could feel the blood rushing out of my head.

"Are you kidding me?" I choked out finally.

Josh, as usual, shut down and didn't say a word. I, on the other hand, could hardly breathe. I was about to unleash the fury, when he had the gall to interrupt me.

"Listen! I know you're upset and I'd love to talk about this, but I have to meet with Pete to give him some documents for a case he's working on."

Pete was a lawyer in their Ituna office. Pete, actually, was the only lawyer in their Ituna office. He was an odd guy, but nice enough.

"HOW CONVENIENT FOR YOU!" I snapped while opening the car door.

I got out as quickly as my fat belly would let me and slammed the door. I tried to resist, but took a quick glance at Josh as I stomped up the driveway. He looked as bad as I felt, which made me feel slightly better, but I was still fuming when I walked into Baba's house.

All those feelings momentarily disappeared, though, when I saw Baba's appearance. She seemed a little less robust. Her cheeks not quite as red and there were dark circles under her eyes. She looked tired and a little sad even.

"Donia!" she said with a little less enthusiasm than usual, but still a bright smile that warmed my angry heart.

"Hey Baba," I greeted her with a sad smile.

"What's wrong?" she asked me in Ukrainian.

I've never been good at concealing my emotions, so I let it all out. I became a snotty, blubbering idiot and, when I was done, I could barely catch my breath. I wasn't sure how Baba would react to my tirade, knowing that she didn't really want me to go in the first place, but she just hugged me and said, "Oy! Oy! Oy!"

Then she went into her cupboard for something and started to brew some magical concoction into a tea, which she placed in my hand after a few minutes. I smelled a floral scent - lavender. I wasn't sure I wanted to drink lavender tea, but Baba looked at me expectantly and so I drank it. Sure enough, I felt much calmer in no time.

Baba then asked me, "Where's Yosh?"

"At the Ituna office," I grumbled, "He needed to give some documents to Pete Zelinski."

"Ees a good boy," was her confusing response.

"WHO? Josh? Or Pete?" I asked.

"Pete! Pete!" she responded, "Ee help his fader with the farming AND ee works as a lawyer AND ee takes his moder to church EVERY Sunday."

"Good for Pete!" was my rather miffed response.

I'm not sure why I was bothered when she went on about Pete. Maybe because I wished she was that enthusiastic about Josh. Or maybe it was because he wore too much hair gel, picked his nose and said stupid things like, "Honest to Pete!" Really how could anybody think this guy was so great?

It was only a few minutes later that "Yosh" walked in with perfect Pete. Baba was more excited than I saw her in a long time.

"Hello Baba!" Pete greeted her with a hug.

This didn't help my already annoyed state with Pete and I was wondering why Josh brought him to Baba's.

As if he were reading my thoughts, Josh answered my question, "I hope this is okay Baba. Pete is going to the same party we're going to later and he was telling me how much he loved your borscht."

"Oh yeah yeah! I'll make some for supper," she happily agreed.

I was beyond annoyed at this point. I knew Josh probably had just brought Pete so he didn't have to hear me gripe at him, but to have my baba make him supper was beyond reasonable. He knew I was not impressed, because he was avoiding my eyes at all costs. To top it all off, Pete and Josh ended up going into the living room to watch hockey. Amazingly, I somehow managed to keep my cool. I didn't want to upset Baba again.

Baba made an amazing feast with borscht, perogies with mushroom sauce, baked salmon, cabbage rolls smothered in butter, onions and tomato sauce, mixed vegetables and homemade bread. As we sat down, she brought out each dish and filled out plates full. When it came to the salmon however, she skipped over me and when straight to Pete. I'm not necessarily the biggest fish fan, but I loved her baked salmon.

"Baba, you missed me," I informed her.

She was busy getting the cabbage rolls, so I figured that she probably didn't hear me at first.

"Baba!" I said a little louder, "You forgot to give me salmon."

"No no!" she finally responded back.

I looked at both Josh and Pete confused.

Then she added, "You shouldn't eet fish!"

I said nothing. I wanted to say something, but I was afraid of what would come out of my mouth if I did, so I said nothing but, "Oh okay."

Josh looked incredibly relieved and Pete, who had no idea what was going on, just looked confused. I ate...and said nothing. It was then that it happened again. Movement! Excited I started to open my mouth to tell Josh, but I stopped myself. Part of me was still so angry at him, but it was at that moment that he gave me one of his looks. It was a look that said I love you, I understand you and I'm sorry all at once, and I knew then that there was no way I could not share this with him. I grabbed his hand silently and put it on my stomach, so he could feel what I was feeling. His eyes got big and were filled with such joy! It was then all my anger dissipated. It was our moment and I was truly happy he was there to share it with me.

He smiled at me knowingly and then said, "Baba! Come feel!"

He grabbed her hand and put it on my stomach. She smiled the biggest smile I had seen in a long time from her. I even let Pete feel my stomach. It was the first time I really felt like my pregnancy was real. I can't explain it, but I was the happiest I'd been in ages.

The party was fun, but your typical Ituna party with the women in the kitchen making food and the men drinking too much in the garage talking about sports, crops and comparing combines. It was good to see everyone. They were excited to hear that I finally felt the baby move. Even Josh made an effort to be sociable. I don't know if it was because Pete was there but, for once, I wasn't embarrassed by his lack of social graces.

At around midnight, the ladies had put out a snack. I filled up my plate and found myself the most comfortable chair I could find. I was amazed that I could eat again after Baba's huge meal. Derrick came and sat beside me with his plate and a bottle of Bohemian beer.

As much as I liked Derrick, his eating manners were less than refined. This happens to be one of my biggest pet peeves, so I tried to not look or listen to him eat, but, unfortunately, he started talking to me.

"So how's your baba?" he said loudly and with his mouth so full of food I could easily identify all four food groups being grinded up into a pulp.

Trying not to look at him too much, I responded with a quick, "She's fine."

With a confused look on his face, he looked at my friend Barb, who was also sitting nearby. She glared at him. The look bothered me.

"Why?" I asked abruptly.

"Oh...just wonderin'," Derrick said awkwardly.

I then looked at Barb who just looked down at her turkey sandwich and said nothing. I tried to finish eating, but I had started to feel tired and irritable. There was a strange tightness across my stomach. I told Josh I wanted to leave and he looked relieved, even though he seemed to be enjoying himself. We left and went back to Baba's.

Lying in the small bed in her extra bedroom, I couldn't fall asleep. The bed was uncomfortable to begin with, but something was bothering me and I couldn't figure it out. I kept thinking back to Derrick and Barb's looks. I chastised myself for not getting more out of them. I decided there was no point in beating myself up over it, so I tried to think of something else.

I could hear that Josh was still awake so I asked him, "Why do you think Baba wouldn't let me eat fish?"

He didn't answer for a second, then came back with, "Maybe she thinks the baby will come out with fins and scales if you do."

I looked at him and then started to giggle. The more Josh told me to stop making so much noise, the louder I got, until it became outright laughter. My laughter must have been infectious, because soon Josh was laughing as well. We laughed until we fell asleep and it was the best sleep I had in ages. I had some pretty weird dreams that night though, but, when I woke up, I couldn't remember any of them.

Don't Decorate the Baby's Room

As the weather got colder, I got larger and, if it was possible, grumpier. However, the situation with Baba was better. She hadn't expelled any "wisdom" on me in over a month. I thought, perhaps, it was because she had given me all the information that she could possibly have to give me by now. I was grateful for this, because the rush of Christmas, school and my over active hormones were getting the best of me. Even Cindy and Janie were on edge around me. If I wasn't barking at my students, I was crying because I burned the chicken or because I ran out of toothpaste. To be honest, I was even getting sick of myself!

"What the hell is wrong with me? Is this normal?" I wailed to Josh one evening when I started crying profusely because of a dog food commercial.

"Hormones?" he offered.

"Nobody is going to want to see the baby after it's born, because they'll all hate me by then," I predicted.

"Don't be ridiculous," he countered, "they understand."

I hoped he was right.

"Maybe I just need some time off. It would have been nice to have done that somewhere nice and warm and sunny!" I pouted.

I still hadn't fully forgiven him for pulling out of the trip and used it to my full advantage as often as possible. He remained silent, but I did hear his deep sigh that usually accompanied him whenever he was feeling stressed out.

I let it go for once and my reward was a backrub. Trying to get off topic as quickly as possible, Josh brought up another one of my favourite topics instead.

"So when do we need to be in Ituna again?" he asked for what seemed like the millionth time.

The man generally had a memory like an elephant when it came to the most ridiculous of things, like what year Thriller came out or when the Battle of Stalingrad took place, but when it came to the stuff that I told him, he couldn't retain anything at all.

"Five!" I replied irritably.

"Oh right! Right!" he answered back somewhat absentmindedly.

The next week was filled with all things Christmassy. Christmas exams, Christmas presents, Christmas tree decorating, Christmas shows and Christmas treats. Although, that was one part of Christmas that I thoroughly enjoyed, especially since I couldn't indulge in Christmas drinks. Even Morales got into the spirit of the season and gave me a hug at the Christmas party and wished me "a very, very, very Merry Christmas." Despite the knowledge that he had indulged in copious amounts of rum and eggnog, I was too shocked to say anything back. I was looking over his shoulder when he hugged me and saw that Janie and Cindy were practically peeing themselves with laughter. Even Josh kept laughing about the "look on my face" and how funny it was.

The one thing that did put a smile on my face was when one of my students, Sophia Yanez, a shy, and somewhat gawky, girl of fifteen, who immigrated with her parents from Chile a few years ago, came to me on the last day of school before Christmas holidays. I was really fond of her for some reason. It was possibly because she reminded me of my baba, and not just because they had the same name. She just looked at me with her big, hazel eyes and didn't say anything at first.

"Yes Sophia?" I asked encouragingly.

She pulled out a gift bag and said embarrassedly, "Here! From my mama and me! For the baby!"

She didn't usually say much, but when she did it was always a delight. She had the sweetest accent.

I was so touched by their thoughtfulness. My first baby gift! I was so excited to see what it was.

"May I open it?" I asked.

"Oh no no!" she insisted, "You must wait!"

"Oh okay then!" I smiled warmly to let her know it was okay, "Well then, tell your mother thank you and I hope your family has a wonderful Christmas."

She gave me a simple "okay" and as I was about to give her a hug, she turned around quickly and booted out of the classroom before she had to say anything else.

I waited until I got home to open the present, because I wanted Josh to be there as well. I waited anxiously for him, but he was late as usual. I was tempted with the idea of just sneaking a peek, but, for once, managed to control myself. Finally, Josh pulled up in his Nissan and I was at the door holding up the present.

"LOOK!" I said excitedly, "Our first baby present!"

"Oh cool!" Josh said enthusiastically, which made me happy because he generally didn't get nearly as excited about receiving gifts as I did.

"I got something too!" he added.

"Really? I wonder what it is?" I pondered, a little peeved that he was stealing my thunder, but, still excited that there was yet another gift.

"A homemade baby quilt!" he answered.

Wait a minute! He opened it without me?!? I was really annoyed now, especially after I had waited for him. The quilt was really beautiful though, so I decided not to harp on about it.

"Who's it from?" I asked.

"Rita Smiley!" he replied.

"I should have guessed!" I laughed.

Rita was always making people things. Her house looked like a ball of yarn threw up in it.

"What's yours?" Josh asked.

"What? Oh! Well look!" I said with a knowing air.

I wasn't about to let on that I didn't know what my present was, even though I knew full well that Rita would have insisted he open the present in front of her, so she could hear him praise her for her beautiful gift. That's just how she was.

I gave the gift bag to Josh anxious to see what it was as well. Josh takes forever to open presents. He was always careful not to rip or tear anything. It was so frustrating to watch. Finally, he pulled out all the tissue paper carefully and pulled the present out. For a brief moment, I wondered if we should actually be looking at it, remembering Baba's concern about getting the baby anything before it's born. I decided that this didn't count as it was a gift. Then I got mad for letting myself go there. Inside was the most beautiful music box I had ever seen. Even Josh was impressed.

"Wow!" he said after a moment.

"Yeah!" I agreed, "It's from Sophia Yanez and her mom. I'm guessing her dad made it though."

Sophia's dad was a carpenter, but in Chile he was a toy maker.

"Lets put it in the baby's room," I suggested.

"Great idea!" Josh agreed.

Somehow in the craziness of work and everything else, we managed to get the baby's room painted and even had a little dresser in there already. I had planned to finish decorating during the holidays. We put it on the dresser. Josh opened it and twisted the knob several times to wind it up. A very sweet melody started to play. It was familiar, but I wasn't sure of the name of the song. I didn't matter though. It was the perfect gift!

We had supper and Josh went over some work while I kept making excuses to go by the baby's room to look at the music box. I kept playing it trying to figure out the name of the song. I was supposed to be wrapping presents and baking for tomorrow's Christmas Eve supper, but I wasn't really in the mood. Besides, I had all the next day.

Of course, the next day came and went too quickly and I ended up rushing around right until the very last minute. Josh was yelling at me to hurry up, because he despised being late more than anything. Finally, we got on the road.

My nerves were a bit on edge. Despite everything going well with Baba lately, I kept remembering our last big family gathering. I tried to relax, but mostly just wanted to throw up. When we got to Baba's house, some of the men were outside trying to figure out how to put up the Christmas lights.

I walked to the typically topsy turvy kitchen and put my almond squares down on the table. I gave my Baba a squeeze from behind and she whipped around and demanded, "Donia! Taste thees borscht!"

Never one to refuse borscht, I complied. As always, it was perfect!

"Yum!" I told her.

"Okay good!" she agreed.

I went through the mass of women to put my coat into the closet. My sister had sat down in the living room and was watching Jeopardy, of all things, with my Uncle Nestor, who was sleeping with his mouth open and snoring loud enough to wake the dead.

"Wassup?" I said in a silly voice.

She giggled and gave me a knowing smile as she raised her glass, "Eggnog!" she stated and broke into a fit of giggles.

I shook my head at her, smiled and started going back into the kitchen, but then, turned around, and turned off the television.

"Hey!" she yelled, "What the hell?"

"Language!" I warned since there were kids around, "Get in the kitchen!" I then commanded.

"Why?" she asked looking genuinely perplexed as to why there would be a need for her to go into the kitchen.

"Get off yer lazy bum and go help for once!" I ordered.

"What am I supposed to do?" she whined.

"Oh for god's sake! Ask them! I'm sure they'll have something for you to do," I smiled condescendingly at her.

She looked pissed off at me, but got up, albeit, begrudgingly. We went into the kitchen and helped prepare the meal. When we all sat down to eat, or really when the men sat down, the women never really sat down for more than a few minutes at a time, I was starving! Usually, Christmas Eve was a day of fasting for us, until the Christmas Eve meal. Being pregnant, I was exempt from that of course, but I had intentionally eaten lightly that day knowing full well I was in for the traditional Christmas Eve meal of twelve meatless dishes.

The first thing we ate, as usual, was honeyed wheat, or kutia. Then we had the borscht. My

Baba, without a doubt, makes the best borscht in the world. It was always the perfect amount of tangy and sweet, which I loved. After those two dishes, we started in on the main meal, which was the traditional Christmas Eve supper and included two types of perogies, mushroom sauce, two types of cabbage rolls, sauerkraut with peas, mashed beans, fish and pickled herring, kolach, pampushky and fruit compote, or funny fruit as we called it. When my Auntie Rose passed me the fish, I knew I had to pass, which I was completely unhappy about, because the fish at Christmas was always so good.

"No thanks!" I said.

Refusing food for Ukrainians, especially at Christmas Eve supper, was pretty much not allowed, so naturally I heard about it.

"You're suppose to eat EVERYTHING!" she told me loudly.

I winced, but shot back quickly, "I'm not allowed to eat fish!"

"Why?" Auntie Rose asked, "You're not allergic are you?"

"No! No!" I replied back and then decided to be cheeky, "Apparently, if I eat fish the baby will come out with fins and scales."

I laughed and there were a few chuckles, but it became familiarly quiet. I could feel my mother glaring at me even from the far end of the table, so I managed to keep my mouth shut for the rest of the meal, but only because I was filling it with the delicious food that was served. I was so stuffed I could hardly move. My Uncle Orest, as usual, had to pull out his home brew and everyone was expected to take a shot. This was one thing I was more than happy to not have to ingest. It was terrible stuff and so strong you could smell it across the room! My uncle didn't quite get the idea that a pregnant woman shouldn't be drinking, so Josh came to my aid by asking for another shot instead.

"Oh great! You're going to be drunk at church!" I gave him a look that said you can stop drinking now.

Normally I didn't care, but since I became pregnant, I had become an alcohol nazi of sorts. Although, I will admit to taking a small sip of the eggnog at our staff Christmas party.

After the meal, we all made our way to church for Christmas Eve mass. It was just down the block, so there was no need to drive. My Uncle Tony drunkenly sang Christmas carols the whole way. The mass was long as usual and I did my best to try and not fall asleep, unlike my Uncle Nestor, who somehow perfected the act of sleeping while standing up. I tried to concentrate on other things like, for instance, why it was that every woman at church, after a certain age, had the same haircut. You know, the important stuff! Tried as hard as I could, but I just couldn't get my mind on the mass. All I could think of was the fact that I wanted to eat more borscht and perogies.

"Jesus!" I thought to myself, "At this rate, I'll be the size of a house by the time I'm in my ninth month. I wonder if I'm having twins!"

It went on and on like this until I caught a glimpse of Baba. I noticed that she looked more tired than usual, but there was still this glow about her. It was hard to explain, she always had this amazing energy about her.

Finally, we were coming close to the end of mass, the congregation was about to start saying the Our Father and it was at that moment the baby decided to take the wind out of me. I had never felt a kick that hard before. I actually doubled over.

Josh looked at me with concern, "You okay?" he asked.

"Yeah," I whispered meekly, "The baby is just pissed that it has to share its' room with the perogies."

Josh started giggling like a drunken school girl. I rolled my eyes at him.

"You're full of them tonight aren't you?" he slurred a bit too loudly.

When church was finally over, we all went back to Baba's house for "lunch" and coffee. I was so tired by then, but still excited for the food. I convinced myself that it was okay because I was eating for two.

It was three in the morning before I got to bed at Baba's after helping clean up and then preparing a bit for the next day's meal. I was a bit irritated, because we wouldn't actually be staying for that meal. We had to go to Josh's parent's house for Christmas supper instead, but I couldn't actually say anything and no one would let me off even if I was six months pregnant.

Waking up the next morning proved to be massively difficult as I didn't sleep well. Baba's mushroom cream sauce did not agree with me at all. Everybody came to the house and we had a "small" breakfast of perogies, cabbage rolls, sausage, wheat and funny fruit. We all squeezed in the living room somehow to open presents. I was excited, because I saw several presents with my name on them. The adults picked names, so it was unusual to have more than one or two presents under the tree.

We all took turns opening our presents, so we could see what everyone received. Personally, I wasn't overly interested in Auntie Olga's new toaster or Uncle Tony's new suspenders, but I didn't want to seem ungrateful, especially when everyone was so generous with the gifts this year. Most of the gifts were for the baby, but Josh did get me a great spa package and my parents gave us money for a snow blower, which made Josh way happier than me. He had been asking for one for the last few years.

When it was all done, I stood up and said with great enthusiasm,

"Thank you everyone for all the wonderful gifts! I can't wait to start decorating the baby's room!"

Suddenly, I saw my mother and Baba whispering furiously back and forth and my Auntie Olga trying to listen in on the conversation. I had noticed my Baba getting kind of irritated, or maybe it was concerned, when we were opening gifts, but couldn't figure out why.

They were speaking in Ukrainian, so I couldn't understand most of what was being said. I cursed myself for not paying more attention in the Ukrainian classes I took when I was younger. Finally, I could see my baba urging my mom to say something and my mom reluctantly agreeing. Baba then got up and went into the kitchen. The aunties, and even some of the uncles, got up to follow.

I looked at my mother expectantly and I could see she really didn't want to say anything, which I think may have been the first for my mom. I finally gave her a look that said, "Enough already! Tell me!" Although, I had a pretty good idea of what she was going to say.

Sure enough, trying to be as good natured and diplomatic as my mother was able to be she spit it out.

"Baba suggests that maybe you should wait until the baby is born to decorate the room," I could tell she wanted to be anywhere but there right at that moment. I felt that familiar feeling of blood rushing to my head again.

"Why?" I curtly asked.

Stupidly, I don't think she was expecting me to ask and I could see she was trying to muster up an adequate answer.

"Well, you know, I mean," she fumbled, and my mother never fumbles, "You should probably make sure everything is okay first."

I became pretty agitated at hearing this, because on top of all the healing and such, my baba claimed that she could see people's futures by reading their tea leaves. A terrible thought emerged of my Baba sneaking my tea cup when I wasn't looking to see what my future held.

"What do you mean?" I anxiously asked.

Josh squeezed my hand to tell me to calm down, but I was having none of it.

I repeated the question, "What do you mean? Does Baba know something? What the hell mom?"

I was near tears and my breathing became a bit laboured.

"No! NO! You know, it's just like the other things she tells you," she said unconvincingly.

I shook my head and went straight into our bed to pack.

"Why?" I asked myself, "Why can't they just let me be happy?"

Josh and I left shortly thereafter and I was so glad to go. I didn't even really feel guilty about thinking that either. I just wanted to go home, but, of course, we still had to go to Josh's parent's house that evening. I rubbed my head and sighed. I really did not want to face any more people, especially family.

As we drove back to Yorkton, I thought about what had happened and a tear slid down my face. Josh squeezed my hand and smiled at me. I forced a smile back, put my head back and closed my eyes.

Don't Go to Cemeteries

I avoided my entire family for the rest of the Christmas break. I even managed to not pick up the phone when my mom called. I knew it would be driving her crazy, but I didn't care. Josh, to his credit, didn't chastise me the way he usually did when I was acting childishly. I think he was worried about the baby more than anything. On my last appointment before Christmas, Dr. Rens expressed concern that the baby was not growing as fast as it should be and gave me a good talking to about my stress levels again. Since then, Josh had been going out of his way to not aggravate me any more than necessary. He saw that I had more than enough frustration with my family. On top of my baba's golden advice, my parents had been driving me crazy with their own ideas about my impending bundle of joy. The latest was about the name of the child. I had been told numerous times to keep the potential names to myself, but in an act of sheer stupidity, I blurted out that we liked the name Isabel.

"Isabel?" my mother questioned.

The tone in her voice was not one of joy or acceptance.

"Yeah! What's wrong with Isabel?" I asked.

"There was a hooker in Ituna named Isabel," was her answer.

I looked at her bewildered for a moment. I wasn't sure if she was being serious or not. It only took a second to tell that she was, indeed, not joking.

"Oh my god mom!!!!" I heaved.

My dad took that moment to pipe in, "It's true!"

"There are no, nor have there ever been, hookers in Ituna!" I barked.

"Oh and you know everything now do you?" my father snidely asked.

"What you're saying is ridiculous and who cares anyway?" I asked exasperatedly.

My mom replied like she hadn't even heard me.

"Do you think you'll be coming over for New Years?" she asked.

"Dammit MOM! We are not talking about New Years!" I said.

"Hey!" my dad warned.

"Is that how you're going to speak in front of the baby?" my mom condescendingly asked.

"Only when you're around!" I scowled at her.

She just sighed.

"So what would you choose then mother?"

I was hoping it wasn't something I actually liked, because I knew she'd tell everyone then that she had picked the name. For once, I got my wish.

"Your dad and I were talking and we thought Elijah would be nice," she answered.

"For a boy?" I asked, confused, since we had been talking about girl's names.

"No. For a girl," she replied.

"Elijah's a boy's name," I replied back

"No it isn't," she said in a haughty tone, "The Boucher's just had a baby and they named her Elijah Faith. Your dad and I thought that would be a great name. You could call her Ellie!"

I could tell she and my father were quite excited by this name, so I was more than happy to burst their bubble.

"Not in a million years! It IS a boy's name and people will always think she is a boy until they meet her. No! It's not happening!"

If I thought that was the end of it, I was wrong. They took any and every opportunity to push their name on us. My sister, of course, was only too happy to join in. Luckily, Josh was definitely on my side with this one.

"Forget it! It's dumb!" was his response when I told him what they thought the girl's name should be.

Luckily, they didn't seem to have a problem with our boy's name. We decided we really liked the name Noah. All through this, I was expecting to hear some superstition about picking out baby names before the baby was born, but, oddly enough, I hadn't heard anything at all from Baba about this.

Regardless, I thought it was best for my own sanity to keep away from everyone for a while. Josh and I spent New Years Day at home with some friends. Since he felt so bad about not taking me on a cruise, he decided to have a Hawaiian themed New Year's party. He organized everything himself. I was so impressed and touched that he would make such an effort, especially since he was so busy at work. He even wore a hula skirt and a coconut bra, which made me laugh so hard I actually threw up a little. I was afraid to ask where he even got them. We had lots of fun and I celebrated with a bit of bubbly at midnight. Josh gave me a dirty look, but I didn't care. Pregnant women drink wine in Europe all the time I thought. What's a few sips of champagne? I did end up feeling a little bad though, which just made me feel weary. I was sick and tired of never being able to do the right thing.

Our friends overstayed their welcome, so I was more than happy to say the last of the goodbyes at four in the morning. I thought about cleaning up, but was so exhausted I went straight to bed. However, I couldn't sleep and it wasn't the usual physical discomfort I felt either. I kept thinking about how I was always letting people control my feelings, instead of being in control of them myself.

I thought to myself, "I can't be letting other people control my well-being."

Since sleep wasn't coming, and all these thoughts were plugging away at my brain non-stop, I got up and cleaned the glasses and dishes that were strewn about the house. We had the bright idea of getting confetti poppers and so our floors looked like disco ball. I had to leave it there though, because the vacuum would have woken up Josh. I was secretly pleased about this, however, because it made our house look nice and sparkly.

It was about six in the morning when I finally finished cleaning up. I went straight to bed and didn't get up until two in the afternoon. Apparently, I missed a call from my mother. I didn't call back.

The day before I had to go back to work, I had another ultrasound. Dr. Rens had wanted to do one after the Christmas break.

I was sitting in the lobby having to pee desperately from all the water they make you drink beforehand. Josh hadn't shown up yet and I was getting more and more worried. I didn't want to go in and find out something was wrong. Not that they told you right then and there, but that didn't stop me from worrying. Josh ran through the door just as they called my name.

Lying on the bed while the ultrasound technician rubbed the gooey clear liquid on my ever expanding belly was not at all enjoyable. She wouldn't tell us anything of course, and we wouldn't find out until the next day at my doctor's appointment. I made lunch plans with the girls to get my mind off my worries. It had been a couple of months since we'd gotten together and I was really looking forward to seeing them.

When I sat down, Angie took one look at me and belted out, "You're huge!"

"Uh, thanks?!" I retorted, somewhat irritated, but mostly amused.

"No problem!" she replied with a huge smirk on her face.

"You really haven't gotten that big," Linda remarked.

They all agreed.

"Really?" I asked, "Because I feel HUGE! Although, I had to have another ultrasound today, because Dr. Rens was concerned after my last visit that the baby wasn't as big as it should be."

"Oh oh!" Sandy responded ominously.

"What?" I replied back a little tensely.

"Oh nothing," she said dismissively.

You could tell that she didn't want to answer, but finally did knowing I wouldn't leave it alone. She proceeded to tell me all about a cousin of hers whose baby didn't grow very big in the womb and then proceeded to have all sort of health issues after it was born, even needing a liver transplant.

As she was telling us all this, I felt my head throbbing. When she was done, I had a full blown headache, a lump in my throat and the familiar tightening chest.

One look at me and Angie just lost it, "Jesus Sandy!" Angie barked, "What the hell is wrong with you? She doesn't need to hear those things! She's obviously worried now!"

Linda grabbed my hand a squeezed it.

"Don't worry about it! Those kinds of problems are rare. It's probably just stress."

Melissa then piped in, "Lets change the subject."

"You think?" Angie retorted.

"Where's your baby shower going to be?" Melissa asked.

The question took me by surprise. I hadn't even really thought about a baby shower yet. I wasn't even sure it was my job to think about that kind of thing.

"Um, not sure," I replied.

"Well, let us know," Linda said.

I sat there a bit hurt, wondering why they weren't offering to have one for me. It made me a little angry actually, especially since I had helped organize showers for all of them.

"Well I'm guessing my friends and family in Ituna will have one for me," I finally said.

"Oh good Lord," Angie complained.

"You mean we will have to go ALL the way there," Sandy whined.

Melissa didn't say anything, although she didn't look really excited either.

"Can't say for sure," I answered tersely, "Don't think it would be fair to ask all of them to come here and then organize everything on top of it all." Melissa must have sensed my annoyance and said to the rest, "It's not that far guys!"

She was met with reluctant acknowledgement and that just served to bother me further. I sighed and changed the conversation.

The rest of lunch was pleasant enough, but I was glad when it was done. I couldn't wait to go home and slip into something comfortable and relax. I was not looking forward to going back to school tomorrow. Luckily, Josh was in a giving mood when he got home and so whatever I asked for, I received. Back rub, foot rub, peanut butter and chocolate ice cream. I felt a lot better.

School went back to normal, which was good in that there wasn't all that added stress of Christmas time activities, but, it also meant Morales was also back to his usual cranky self. He even bellowed at me in front of students that first day back. Normally, this would have sent me into a tizzy and I would have needed a TR meeting with Janie and Cindy, but I had decided my New Year's resolution was to try to be the zen like person I've always wanted to be. It wasn't easy, but I somehow managed to just smile at him, which enjoyably, caught him off guard a bit and made him leave abruptly.

I had my doctor's appointment right after school. By then, I had that familiar strained feeling in my head. I kept praying to God that everything would be okay. I must have said a hundred Hail Mary's.

When Dr. Rens walked in, he was smiling and I immediately relaxed.

"So things are looking better!" he told me in his yummy South African accent.

"Oh thank goodness!" I replied.

Josh let out a deep breath, like he had been holding it up until that point.

"Just continue to keep the stress levels down and take care of yourself. Remember to eat!" he said with mock sternness.

Like that has ever been a problem!

He did a routine check up and then we left. Josh was so happy, he actually decided to play hooky and didn't go back to work. We got Chinese take out and rented a romantic comedy and cuddled on our big, plush sofa. It was a great night!

The next day went great as well. My students were behaving well. Morales didn't get on my case or nerves. When I got home, I decided to make Josh's favourite - spaghetti and meatballs. I even made him the disgusting canned meat sauce that he, for some unfathomable reason, loved so much.

The phone rang while I was cooking. I looked at the caller - my mother. I debated not answering. The day was going so well after all, but I ultimately decided I couldn't ignore her forever and that our uncommunicative state had probably gone on long enough, so I picked up the phone.

"Helllooo!" I said cheerfully as possible.

"Well it's about time!" was her aggravated reply.

I sighed and immediately regretted my decision.

"I'm sorry!" I said truthfully, "I think I just needed a break."

She went on for a bit about how insensitive I was being to HER! I tuned out after a minute and concentrated on the spaghetti.

She finally lost her steam and asked, "How was your ultrasound?"

Happy for the subject change, I told her all about my appointment. You could tell she was relieved.

"I was praying for you so much!" she said.

I laughed a little.

"Yeah I was praying for me too!"

It was at that moment, for the very first time ever, I saw a bit of my mother in myself. I then remembered that I needed to ask her about going to Ituna for my Gido's annual blessing at the cemetery.

"So, off topic here, but what time is Gido's blessing going to be?" I asked.

Every year we went to his grave with a priest and did a blessing of the departed souls ceremony. We had been doing it for twenty years and I had never missed going.

My mother didn't answer right away and then said, "Maybe you should stay home this year...if you're not feeling well."

"What are you talking about mom? I feel fine and the baby is fine! Why wouldn't I come?" I asked.

"Oh I don't know," she answered sheepishly.

"Oh oh," I thought to myself.

"Okay what's up?" I demanded firmly.

After another lengthy pause, she finally replied, "Well Baba thought maybe you shouldn't come."

I knew it!

"And why is that?" I asked in a not too friendly voice.

She chose her words carefully, "Well, I guess it may not be in your best interest to go to a cemetery."

I was incredulous. Seriously? This was taking it too far and in one instant she had burst my happy little bubble. I completely lost it.

"There is no damn way I'm not going!" I yelled and continued to do so for another ten minutes.

"Okay! Okay! Fine go!" she said when she was finally able to speak. Probably just to get me to shut up.

I was still fuming when Josh got home. I told him what happened. Unfortunately, along with the news that everything was okay with the baby, his sympathetic nature had vanished.

"Why do you get so upset?" he questioned me, "Just ignore her!"

"Easy for you to say!" I snapped, but I left it there.

Zen, I reminded myself. Just...zen!

We went to Ituna with my parents and my sister, who looked half dead herself.

"Late night?" I inquired with a smirk.

She groaned and in a barely audible voice let out, "Goooodddd! My head!"

"Nice," I replied shaking my head.

When we got to Baba's, I hugged her, but she didn't really hug me back. In fact, she did her best, or so it seemed, to ignore me. She kept busy preparing lunch for everyone. The usual guests were there and I chatted with everyone.

After lunch, it was time to go. However, Baba and my mother were missing. Finally, we could hear some voices arguing in Baba's bedroom. Unfortunately, the door was closed, so it was hard to hear what was being said.

I walked into Baba's bedroom. The tension was thick in there. Baba muttered something in Ukrainian, which I mostly didn't understand, except for the last two words. "Ni dobre!"

No good!

No good?

"What?" I simply said to my mother.

My Baba walked out of the room.

"Close the door," she ordered.

I closed the door and my mom spoke.

"Baba, simply put, doesn't want you to come."

I shook my head, "Jesus Christ Mom!"

"Emma!" she reproached me.

"Well!!!"

Like this was all the explanation I needed, because the whole thing was so insane, what else could you say?

"I know you have mentioned, that I should be more respectful of her beliefs, but, quite honestly, I have had enough this silliness and stupidity. I really have," I announced.

"I know!" she replied back bluntly.

"So, what now? I can't go?" I whined.

She shook her head.

"Seriously! This is such bullshit!" I complained loudly, "Like no woman in the history of the universe has gone to a cemetery while pregnant and not come out of it normal!"

"Tykho!" my mother snapped, "Keep your voice down!"

My dad came in at that moment.

"They're leaving," he announced.

"Oh great!" I replied flopping teary eyed onto the bed, "So what am I suppose to do?"

Dad put his hand on my shoulder and smiled weakly, but with empathy.

"You go," he told my mom, "I'll stay with her."

My mom didn't argue and left the house with her arm wrapped around Josh's arm. If I wasn't feeling so sorry for myself, I'd have felt sorry for him.

I was about to take my coat off, when my dad said, "Let's go for a walk."

I put my coat back on and went to the back door to get my boots.

My dad and I had this weird relationship, I knew he cared greatly for me, but he usually had a hard time showing it. We tended to fight a lot, but, on the other hand, he could also be great fun! We were a lot alike, as much as I hated to admit it.

We didn't say a lot for the first few minutes. Mostly small talk. It was a beautiful day, which was odd for January in Saskatchewan. Usually it was -30 Celsius, but that day it was only -5 and it was sunny and bright with no wind, which made for great walking weather.

We walked to the cafe and picked up two coffees. While we made our way back, my dad said, "You know Emma, your baba loves you very much."

"I know she does," I replied back, "But all these crazy rules that I'm supposed to follow have made me insane!"

I was getting tired of this same old argument and my same old response.

"It's just the old ways," he answered back calmly.

"Yes I know dad!" I said not so calmly, "But WHY hasn't anybody bothered to explain the new ways to all these old Ukrainians? " I half-joked, "Also," I added, "Most of it makes NO SENSE!"

"It's not that simple," he responded, "If I asked you why you have to blink 5 times when you see the clock turn 11:11, could you explain it?" I now regretted telling my father about my quirky idiosyncrasy. "This is what she was brought up to believe. Silly or not, you have to respect that."

I pondered this for a moment, and then replied,

"Yes and that's all fine and well, but the fact is she's pushing her ideas onto me, and even though I know they're irrational, I still find myself pausing before I put a necklace on or when I go to buy something for the baby. It's endless!! I'm already an anxious person. I don't need these added worries. I really don't," I explained.

My dad smiled and put his arm around me, "I know, but your baba is getting older you know," he paused as to think of what to say next, "her health...well you know what it's like when you get older."

"No!" I teased, "What's it like dad?"

"Well you start losing your hair, your hearing, your eyesight! Te dah!" he teased back.

I laughed heartily and noticed somehow we had made our way to the cemetery. Well, not the cemetery per se, but the outer edges. We stood behind a tree where no one could see us. I stood in silence for a few minutes. It was difficult to make out what the priest and everyone was saying, so I just said a little prayer for my gido. When I was done I looked at my dad and said, "You know you can go if you want."

"No, no!" he replied a little too quickly, "I'm fine!"

I secretly think he was happy not to have to go, AGAIN, to this service, so we just walked back to Baba's and waited for the others to return.

Don't Show the Baby to Strangers for Forty Days

January had passed quickly thank goodness. There was at least three weeks of -35 to -40 below weather. Nothing any person who was raised in Saskatchewan wasn't accustomed to, but when you were as big as a whale, it could make for some pretty uncomfortable situations. For one, I couldn't close my winter jacket, and I refused Josh's suggestion of buying a bigger one. Bending over to put on my boots was also proving to be very difficult. Physically I was a mess! Mentally though, I was more calm than I had been in ages.

Despite the conversation with my dad, I realized that avoidance was the only thing that kept me sane and my stress levels down. One trip to the doctor was all the convincing I needed.

"The baby's a good size now. Well within average for this time," he remarked, "And you seem so much more relaxed. Your blood pressure is down as well."

"That's good," I replied calmly.

"What are you doing differently?" he inquired.

I took a second to figure out how to answer that question. Telling him that I was avoiding speaking to my family, especially my mother and Baba, did not really sound very nice, so I just said, "Avoiding, uh, stressful situations."

He smiled and patted me on the head as if to say "good girl" like I was dog and walked out of the examination room without saying goodbye. I smiled until he left the room and then sighed. One of those deep, long sighs that lets out all the tension. All this zen was hard work! The thing is that I did feel bad. My baba had called a few times and I never called back.

I got my mom to tell her that I was just really busy with school right now, which wasn't a complete lie, as finals were keeping me occupied. My mom called me every day and, for the most part, I didn't call her back either. Of course, that didn't stop her from coming over and bitching at me for not answering the phone, but it was a lot less than usual. I spent most of my time now just trying not to go off the edge like I had before. I had convinced myself that it was the only way to cope, even though it didn't really feel quite right to me either.

"I wish I was like you," I said to Josh one night after supper.

"Wait! Where's the video camera?" he teased.

This was not something he had ever expected to hear from me. Usually I was telling him he should be more like me.

"You can let things go. Nothing seems to upset or rattle you," I explained, "For me, it's all up here," I pointed to my head, "Twisting my mind around and making me fricking crazy!!"

"You just need to not let everything bother and worry you so much," he stated matter-of-factly like I hadn't heard him say this a millions times before.

"Oh REALLY? Is that all?" I answered back sarcastically, "Why didn't you tell me this before? Everything would have worked out SO much better!"

"Ha ha!" was his annoyed reply.

I shook my head and became serious, "I really, really wish I could."

Deanna called me at the end of January.

"Hey there!" she greeted me loudly.

"Hey! Why are you yelling," I asked.

"Kids!" was her answer, like that should explain everything.

She must have sensed my confusion and added, "You'll understand soon enough."

"Ah okay then! Can't wait!" I said with mock enthusiasm.

"So are your fancy city friends putting on a big, baby shindig for you?" she asked.

"Uh no!" I said embarrassed by my answer.

"Well, we'd like to put on something for you then," she replied enthusiastically.

"I don't want to put you out," I said feeling guilty that my fancy city friends were being so lame.

"No, no!" she answered, "We're happy to do it! Most of your family lives here anyways and you can invite those city girls too if you'd like," she told me.

"Well thanks," I replied warmly," I really appreciate that."

"So when is good for you?" she asked, "Would you like it before the baby is born or after?"

I thought about it for a second.

"Maybe after?" I pondered aloud, "You know otherwise my baba will be all stressed because we're giving the baby stuff before it's born," I joked.

"Oh yeah!" she chuckled meekly like she was uncomfortable.

"Let me get back to you on that!" I told her.

"Okay!" she replied, "Talk soon then!"

After she hung up, I knew I'd have to call my mother. It had been a while since I last called her and I wasn't looking forward to her reaction. I took a deep breath and dialled the phone.

"Hawlo!" she answered sounding exactly like Baba.

"Hi!" I said back somewhat sheepishly.

"Ho ho ho!" she responded sounding like Santa Claus, "Look who's gracing me with a phone call. Hello to you your highness."

"Mom! Come on!" I pleaded.

"What do you need?" she snapped, "I'm baking!"

I was taken aback by her response. I knew she'd be pissed, but my mother didn't generally hold a grudge. I tried not to react.

"Deanna called," I told her, "She's going to put on baby shower for me, but wants to know when it should be."

She didn't respond.

"Mom?" I called wondering if she had hung up on me.

"Yeah, yeah! I'm listening," she snapped again.

"If this isn't a good time," I started, but was cut off by her.

"You should probably ask Baba," she sighed.

"Can't you ask her?" I asked.

"Emma!" she snarled, "You have been ignoring everyone that cares about you for the last month. Now when it comes time for something YOU want, you expect everyone to now come running to your side? You can't treat people, especially your Baba, that way and not expect any repercussions. Look I know you're pregnant and your hormones have gotten a little crazy and things often seem worse than they really are. And I know that Baba

180

can be a bit much sometimes and she made you worry and I know I nag you a lot, but that's NO EXCUSE for turning your back on us! You want something? Do it yourself!"

With that she hung up on me! I felt like I had been hit by a bus. It takes a lot for my mom to explode that badly. I just sat there for a while collecting my senses. I was still shaking when I picked up the phone again and slowly dialled. I was praying that no one would answer, but finally I heard the phone being picked up. It took some time, though, for Baba to answer.

"Baba?" I called wondering why there was no answer.

"Oh Donia!" she said breathlessly.

"Baba are you okay?" I anxiously asked.

"Um hm!" she mumbled, "I was just having nap."

"Oh," I replied.

I didn't say anything for a few seconds, because I was unsure of how to start.

"Baba," I began, "I'm really sorry I haven't spoken to you in a long time."

"Yeah, yeah!" she answered weakly, "Ees okay!"

"No not really," I admitted, trying to decide if I should explain why.

I decided not and just went with the reason I called.

I explained what was going on and ended by, "I know you don't really feel we should be giving the baby anything until after it's born. So I was wondering if we should have the shower after the baby is born?" I asked, "How does that work for you?"

It took her awhile to reply, but then answered, "Oh Donia, have eet before! The baby shouldn't see strangers for forty days after it's born, so have eet before," was her reply.

I laughed to myself a bit over her response, but something told me I should follow her advice, even if it was bit contradictory.

"Okay then Baba. Thank-you! I'll let you know when it is, okay?" I told her.

"Okay Donia," she replied again breathlessly, "I go!"

"Okay Baba, I love..," but she hung up before I could finish.

I sat there again wondering what to do. It was obvious my Baba wasn't well, but I wasn't about to call my mom again, so I called Deanna back and told her we could set the date before the baby arrived.

"Okey dokes!" she chirped.

I didn't know how to broach the next thing I wanted to say, so I decided to bring up the subject casually.

"You know my baba seemed pretty out of breath. I'm a bit worried about her. Don't suppose you or your mom could check on her tomorrow by any chance?" I asked.

Deanna paused before she answered,

"Oh sure! She's just been a little under the weather lately. Don't worry about it! I'm sure she's fine."

I didn't know how to respond to this. I was, on one hand, angry at my mother for not telling me, especially when everyone clearly knew what was going on with her. On the other hand, I was mostly angry at myself, and ashamed for not being there for my baba. It wasn't like I hadn't seen her turn for the worse.

"Thanks!" I replied and then added, "Gotta go actually. Talk soon!"

I had to get off the phone as quickly as possible before I started crying. That whole night I could barely sleep. I was plagued by worry, anger and anxiety. The next morning, as I was getting ready for work, I tried calling Baba three times, but there was no answer.

By lunch I was ready to have a meltdown. Even Morales asked me if I was okay. The minute I got home, I tried calling again but to avail. I had a brief thought that maybe something had happened. I knew I had to bite the bullet and call my mother again. I called the house, but there was no answer there either.

"Dammit anyway," I muttered to myself, "Where the hell is everyone?"

I then tried my mom's cell phone. It rang and rang and then, finally, I heard her pick it up.

"Hello!" she answered.

"Mom!" I said forcefully, "Have you spoken to Baba today?"

"I'm with her actually," she replied nonchalantly.

"What?" I said worriedly, "Why?"

"Mr. Blazieko died and the funeral was this morning," she answered.

"Why didn't you tell me??" I asked indignantly.

"For one to know things, one must first pick up the phone," she said patronizingly.

"Well I've been trying to call her ALL day," I responded smugly.

"Now you know how it feels," she said with dramatic emphasis.

For the second time in as many days, I was taken aback by her response. Was she saying that Baba didn't answer on purpose? I could see my mom being catty, but Baba?

I let out a sound that let her know of my frustration and displeasure of her response.

"Is she okay?" I gritted my teeth.

"She is fine," was her concise response, then, "The family is coming over and we're making supper, so I have to go. Toodles."

Toodles?

I wasn't sure how I felt, because while I was relieved to hear my baba was okay, my mother's haughty manner and the thought that my baba would purposely ignore me left a bitter taste in my mouth. Even worse, I couldn't help but feel that I was getting a taste of my own medicine and I totally deserved being treated this way.

I chose not to tell Josh as I knew he'd probably have no sympathy for me and, most likely, deservedly so. I decided to leave things alone and hoped against hope that everything would be okay in time for the baby shower next month.

Fortunately, the month passed quickly. I had only spoken to my baba a few times. My mother and I spoke more often, but it felt different somehow. It felt like maybe the joy of being a first time grandmother was taken away, because I had been so awful to Baba, her mother. I was not sure if that made any sense, but that's how it felt. I prayed everything would go back to normal after the shower.

The day of the shower came and I drove up that Saturday afternoon with my mom and sister. I tried to make conversation, but neither of them were very talkative. My sister had been out late the night before and just wanted to sleep, and my mom just seemed like she had other things on her mind. I decided to leave it alone and tried to enjoy the silence not wanting any bad feelings to disrupt the day.

When we pulled up to Deanna's house, my mom left the car running.

"Why aren't you turning the car off?" I asked.

"I have to go see mom first," she said.

"Baba? I thought Auntie Olga was bringing her," I replied.

"No, uh, no!" she simply said without any more explanation.

Krissy started whining about the cold, so even though I wanted to find out more, I couldn't.

"Okay then! See you in a bit?" I asked.

"Uh huh," my mom responded noncommittally.

I got out and she drove off.

"Weird!" I said to Krissy.

"Hmm," she managed as she was busy texting.

"Put that away!" I demanded.

She, of course, ignored me, but by this point, it didn't matter because Deanna had answered the door.

Thirty eight women came to my shower and I had no idea who some of them even were. There was so and so's mother, or some distant cousin who lives in town. I wasn't sure why they were there, but I wasn't about to complain. I was trying to focus on what was happening around me - the food, the decorations, the silly shower games, but I kept looking at the door to see if my mom and Baba were there yet.

Finally, as we were about to sit down to open presents, my mother walked in...without Baba. I stood up quickly when she walked in, ready to go to Baba and give her a hug, but the moment I saw that she wasn't there I sat back down dejectedly.

"Where's Baba?" I asked trying to put on a brave face.

Everyone looked uncomfortable. It felt like they were all in on this secret and I was the only jerk who didn't know what was going on.

"She had a headache," she replied.

"Had?" I said confused.

"HAS! Has!" she vigorously corrected herself.

"Oh!" I felt an extreme sadness come over me.

I couldn't really enjoy the company, the gifts, the food. All of it was lovely, but it was so hard to fake being happy. I was glad when the shower was over.

As we were leaving the house, Deanna hugged me.

"Thank you SO much!" I said with as much enthusiasm as I could muster.

"You okay?" she looked concerned.

"Yep!" I simply replied, not wanting to break down and cry.

The moment we got all the presents in the car, along with the balloons, streamers and Deanna's mom's cinnamon buns, I faced my mom and demanded that she take me to see Baba.

"Oh I don't know honey," she said cautiously.

"NOW!" I demanded once again even more fiercely.

Even my sister looked concerned at this point and I think my mother knew I was not taking no for an answer, so she drove to Baba's. I opened the car door before she even stopped and moved my big belly up her driveway and into her house as fast as I could. I turned to look at the car for a brief second, before turning to go to the back of the house. I could see my sister's hand pressed against the frosted window trying to make footprint patterns. I went into the house shyly, suddenly feeling a bit awkward.

"Baba?" I called out.

"Hawlo?" I heard her weak voice coming from her bedroom.

There were no lights on so it was dark, but I could still see her body well enough to be shocked at her appearance. She had lost so much weight in so little time. Her usual plump face looked gaunt and sickly. I didn't know what to say at first. Gulping hard and trying not to break down and make her feel bad, I finally managed a warm hello.

"Hello Donia!" she seemed embarrassed for me to see her like that which made it even harder not to lose control of myself.

I kneeled down beside her bed and touched her sunken cheek and then grabbed her hand.

"I missed you today," I told her with great sadness.

She looked at me for a moment staring and that look hit me so hard. It was the look of surrender and it scared the hell out of me.

"I'm sorry I meesed your party," she apologized.

"Me too!" I choked out.

I was teary eyed by now.

"Shhh! Shhh!" she whispered wiping my eyes lovingly.

I wanted to say more, I needed to say more, but she closed her eyes and fell asleep. I watched her for a bit until I felt satisfied that she was indeed just sleeping. I got up and kissed her on the cheek and left.

Nothing was said on the way home. My tears didn't stop though and I could see my mom was concerned. At one point she grabbed my hand and gave it a squeeze. I held on and wouldn't let go.

When I got home and into the house with all those presents. I went into Josh's arms and just cried and cried until there were no more tears. I knew he was confused, but he didn't say a word.

One week later, I got a call to come down to the office, "Phone call!" the secretary said.

I picked up the phone and listened to the terrible words on the other line.

Early March - A Goodbye and a Hello

I dropped the phone or, at least, that's what I was told. Everything went completely black. I couldn't breathe. My heart was pounding really hard and fast and my whole body went stiff. I couldn't hear anything.

The next thing I knew is that I woke up in the hospital confused and a bit scared. My head hurt a lot. I looked over and saw Josh looking pale himself. He grabbed my hand and asked if I was okay. I didn't know how to answer. Was I okay? What happened? Was I dreaming? My mind had a million things going through it and it made my head hurt even more.

"I...don't...know!" I finally blurted out.

I asked him what happened and he told me.

"So it's true?" I asked him, "Baba died?"

"Yes," answered, "Honey I'm so sorry."

I felt my body tense up again. Dr. Rens came in and explained that they did some tests and everything was okay and that I had a severe anxiety attack.

"It felt like a heart attack!" I retorted.

"Many people say that," he replied back, "Just take her easy for a few days," he commanded, "I want you on bed rest."

"What about work?" Josh asked.

"I'll write you a note, so you can go on stress leave," Dr. Rens answered.

I was so relieved. The last thing I wanted to do is go back to work. Josh took me home and my dad came over. He looked pretty rough and I could see he was really worried about me.

"Mom's sorry she can't be here," he first said.

"Don't worry about it Dad," I replied.

"She's helping make arrangements," he went on.

"I know!" I said a bit tensely.

I didn't really want to talk about it.

My dad looked unsure of what to say next, so I helped him out and offered, "If they need any help."

"No, no," he countered, "You just get better. That's what Baba would have wanted."

Those words stung, but I agreed. I couldn't imagine helping out anyway. Somehow that would have made it real.

Baba's funeral was on the Saturday after she died. Josh and I drove up that morning. I hadn't seen or spoken to anyone, except my dad, in that time. I wasn't sure how I would handle it, and I was worried I'd have another anxiety attack.

 The service was a typical Ukrainian Catholic service. Really long and really Ukrainian. I stood there numb, trying not to look at the coffin which was left open. I felt like if I looked, I would explode. However, there came a point where the whole family came up to offer their final goodbyes. My feet felt like cement, but Josh held my hand and pulled me to that place that I didn't want to go. It wasn't until I got right in front of the casket that I actually looked at her. I was surprised to feel no anxiety at all. She looked so peaceful and beautiful. My heart warmed a little at the thought of how Baba was now in Heaven. probably making God some perogies. I leaned over put my hand on her cheek and whispered in her ear, "Goodbye Baba!"

When the service was over and they closed the casket, I broke down. I would never see my baba again. The walk down the church was the hardest walk I had ever taken and when they lowered her into the ground, I wanted to jump in after her. My head kept screaming NO NO NO!!!!! I felt like a part of me died that day.

There was a lunch at the church hall afterwards, but I couldn't eat, despite my family's best efforts. I just felt numb and my head felt like it was floating above the rest of my body. I spoke to people who spoke to me, but I never really knew what was said. Sympathies and condolences I imagine.

As I was sitting in the hall though, I noticed how all of my friends and all of my family were working together, laughing together and crying together. That sense of community and fellowship and the love they had for each other was so strong. I felt a twinge of envy at seeing this, and maybe some guilt. I mocked these small town people many times, but I never really understood the value of living in a small town until that moment. I was so happy that Baba had so much love and support in her life.

We went back to Baba's house afterwards, just the family. I sat quietly and listened and laughed at all the stories I heard from my aunts and uncles and cousins about my Baba. Of course, there was more food. This time I ate. I sat down in a chair in the living room with all of my aunties. They were talking to me about their pregnancies and I listened to their wonderful stories. I asked with absolutely no bitterness or sarcasm, "Did you get "advice" from Baba too?"

They all laughed.

"And how!" Auntie Katherine exclaimed.

They told me all the same things that Baba had told me not to do as well and even shared a few new ones with me. Then Auntie Rose became serious with me for a second.

"You know why she said all those things to you right?" she asked, "She was just trying to protect your baby."

I looked at her confused. Somehow, I had never thought about it like that before.

"Protect my baby?" I replied.

My auntie went on to tell me of the babies Baba had lost and how her mother had sent her a letter of all the things she must do to keep her children safe from harm. She followed those rules religiously and no child of hers after that ever came into harm's way.

"You're kidding?" I asked incredulously, "She thought it was because of these rules?"

"Yes, yes! They were very superstitious in the old country," Auntie Olga replied.

"No kidding!" I agreed.

I felt that familiar tension again.

"I was so terrible to her," I admitted ashamedly, "I feel like I caused her to be sick."

I tried to swallow my food, but it wouldn't go down my throat. All my aunties started talking at once.

"No! No! No!"

"Baba loved you so much!"

"She was never, ever mad at you!"

"She had health problems for a long time."

It was nice of them to say, but I had felt they were just trying to make me feel better.

When it was time to leave, I gave absolutely everyone a hug. When I got to my mom, I held her the longest. When we let go, I saw tears in her eyes and, more importantly, forgiveness. It was at that moment that I felt a great wave of love rush through me for my mom. More than I had felt in a long time. I told her right then that I loved her.

I held Josh's hand all the way home until about ten minutes out of Yorkton. Quite abruptly, I felt a quite intense pain. I had been having Braxton Hicks pains for a few weeks now, but this felt different somehow.

"Ow!" I grimaced taking my hand that was holding Josh's hand and putting it on my stomach.

"What?" Josh asked alarmed.

"Just a pain," I disregarded it.

"Well it can't be labour right?" he asked, "You're only 37 weeks!" he sounded nervous.

I informed him that a woman could safely have a baby after 37 weeks. I don't think that comforted him. After a while I felt another pain.

"How far apart was that?" I asked.

"I don't know," he answered excitedly.

"I wasn't really paying attention to the time. Should we be going to the hospital?" his voice was getting a bit high.

"No I'm fine," I answered, but wasn't really sure if that was true.

We went home, but the pains didn't go away. They just became worse and worse. By four a.m., I couldn't stand it any longer.

"Hospital! NOW!" I commanded through the pain and clenched teeth.

They ask you about a thousand questions when you get to the hospital and it was all I could do from strangling someone.

"Yes I want drugs! Now leave me alone and get this thing out of me!" I wanted to yell.

When we got to obstetrics, they put me on a fetal monitoring machine, which was extremely uncomfortable, but it was cool to see the big waves every time I had a labour pain, or, at least, it would have been if I hadn't been in so much bloody pain!

When they told me I was only five centimetres dilated, I could have cried.

"Can I have something for the pain?" I asked.

"Sure!" the nurse answered.

More beautiful words had never been spoken.

They also suggested taking a bath. I wasn't convinced that would help anything, but I figured I'd give it a try. After an hour and half and still no drugs, I noticed something besides my shrivelled up fingers. My pain had subsided greatly. I could actually barely feel them anymore.

Finally, the nurse came back, but told me that I had to go back on the fetal monitor again. I looked at Josh tiredly. It was so nice and comfortable in that warm bath, but I did what I was told.

As I was getting out of the tub, I remembered that we hadn't called our parents yet, so I made sure Josh informed them of what was happening while I was being hooked up to the monitor.

When he got back, I was strapped down.

Almost as soon as I got out of the bath, the contractions started getting strong again, but when the nurse came to check on me she said, "Only seven centimetres."

I groaned.

After half an hour, they took me off the monitor and I went straight back into the glorious tub, except, this time, it didn't feel as glorious.

"Oh shit! Oh god! Ohhhhhhhhhh!!" I could barely breath. It hurt so bad. I can't even describe the pain. I kept thinking of how unfair it was that men didn't have to go through all this. It got to the point where I literally could not handle the agony anymore. The stronger the pain got, the nastier, I'm embarrassed to say, my language became.

"Get someone!" I demanded.

The nurse came and calmly said, "Ok let's check you again."

This time I was ready to go. I couldn't decide if this made me happy or not.

I couldn't believe how many people were around me. All these doctors and nurses. Without prompting, I started to bear down.

One of the nurses noticed and snapped, "Are you pushing?"

A little scared at her reaction, I replied meekly, "No?!"

I tried to change the subject by asking, "When am I getting my epidural?"

"Oh honey," said the same nurse, trying and failing miserably, to sound remorseful, "It's too late!"

I was NOT happy to hear that at all.

The next hour was not what you'd call pleasant. Doctors, nurses, metal contraptions, rubber gloves, blood, push, PUUUUSHHH!! Josh tried to be comforting, but he was just aggravating me mostly. At some point, I could hear my mom outside the room pestering the doctors who went outside for a minute for a quick consult. The baby wasn't coming out as easily as they hoped and they were deciding whether to proceed with a C-section or not. They came back and decided on an episiotomy. It was only ten minutes after that when I became a mother to a beautiful baby girl. I couldn't believe that this amazing creature had just been inside me. I never wanted to let her go!! I was so tired. I smelled pretty funky. I mistakenly thought it was over, but they still had to pull out my placenta and stitch me up. I gave the baby to Josh, unwillingly, while they finished up.

When I was done, Josh handed the baby back to me and laid down beside me. We stared at her in awe. He kissed my forehead.

"Hi mommy!" he sweetly said and smiled at me.

"Hi daddy!" I smiled back at him.

"WOW!" he finally let out.

"I KNOW!" I agreed, "CRAZY!"

The nurse had told me to try feeding as soon as possible and so I attempted to do that, but she just wanted to snuggle beside me and sleep, so I gave up pretty quickly. I was just so very happy and so very, very tired, but I couldn't help but sit there and stare at her, loving her and relishing in what had just happened.

Finally, my mom came in and she put her hand on the baby's head ever so gently and she smiled. It was wonderful to see. I hadn't seen my mom smile in quite some time. She put a gift bag down on the table beside me.

"What's that?" I asked.

She looked at me and then the baby and smiled warmly. Without saying a word, she picked up the bag and gave it to me. I opened it and in it was the most gorgeous, tiny knitted sweater I had ever seen in a delicate pink.

"Oh mom!" I exclaimed, "It's beautiful! Thank you!"

She smiled again and said, "Actually, it's not from me."

I looked at her confused.

"Who then?" I asked.

She pulled a card out of the bag that I had missed. When I read it, I was absolutely floored.

Dear Donia,
I am so proud of the woman you have become. So strong and so independent. I am sorry for upsetting you. You know Baba, she is so old and forgetful. You know that I love you with all of my heart. I am very excited to meet my great grand daughter.
Love,
Baba

A lump formed in my throat, I could barely speak. Tears welled up in my eyes. Josh looked at me concerned.

Finally I spit out, "But..how..how did she..know?"

My mom laughed a bit and said, "Well she said she knew because you had thick ankles!"

I looked at my mom for a second and then started to laugh with her. Josh joined in as well. We laughed long and hard and it felt good. As I looked down at my beautiful little girl, I touched her big, red, round cheeks that immediately felt so familiar and I knew. I knew the name we had chosen would not do and that her name had chosen her. I looked at Josh and I could see he knew as well.

I looked back down at my little angel and kissed her on her cheek and whispered in her little ear, "Hello Sophia!"

Made in the USA
Middletown, DE
25 March 2017